TABLE OF CONTENTS

Prologue

PROLOGUE

Dr. Beckett Conroy.
Executive Chairman,
Hera-soter Establishment Committee.
Project Establishment Log.
02-30-04. FE

—the enemy has surrounded the command pod. It is beginning to look as though they may overwhelm us.....

*

Day-five, Week-three, Year, Zero-one.

Hera-soter is a paradise of lush, greenish-blue vegetation, short ankle-high red-colored grass and beautiful dark-blue lakes of pristine water. There are several low-level mountain ranges on various parts of the planet, the highest of which is about seven thousand meters. It is hard to believe we have found a planet so similar to Earth, be it with a few quirky differences.

THE BEAUTIFUL PLANET

BY

COLIN SETTERFIELD

SURVIVAL OF A SPECIES

Part Three

ISBN 978-1-988719-08-5

My late arrival with the android, Lieutenant Sparkle and the alien Ossimantus, trailed the Andromeda's main compliment by two months. Our craft will remain in low, planet orbit for posterity as a museum, dedicated to the Human Relocation Project. It will be a testimony to the success of the first mission. Earth still occupies our minds but almost everyone is now normalized to the constraints of our new home—Hera-soter.

Fifty-one light years distant from Earth and within the scope of the Pegasus constellation, our new planet is an esthetic Nirvana with everything we need to survive as a species, but dangers also abound. Our center of our main camp, or village, still embraces the escape pods in which the remainder of the Andromeda's compliment arrived on the planet, after the Crustan attack. With some ingenuity from our resident engineers we have erected a host of small homes, with the use of local soil, rock and timber, to house our numbers.

The Andromeda's original compliment of 1265, lessened by the Crustan attack before our arrival, left the new colony with 729 inhabitants. 538 people perished when our refurbished spaceship, on its maiden voyage from Earth, came under Alien fire—Lieutenant Sparkle and I ejected the damaged pods with the remains of our dead and sent them on an endless journey into deep space. Inclusive of two infant births since our arrival, twelve people have succumbed to the many resident dangers. Our total human compliment is now 719.

Before we left Earth, the plan to relocate our species to a new habitat contained certain dates when the next trans-terrestrial ship would arrive with another group of pioneers, among them my father and his young wife, Freda. And so, life on Hera-soter goes on each day, a gift of providence we are all grateful for.

∞∞

ONE

The Forest Dwellers

"Get down and don't make a sound," I said.

Carla knelt and clutched the stout stick as she peered through the knee-high grass.

"What is it, hon?"

I indicated to a large tree. "A family of forest dwellers. They haven't seen us yet, so lie still."

She raised herself up to gain a better view and gazed at the indicated area.

"Oh look at the babies—they're so sweet."

I chuckled at her comment. Out on a walk alone the two of us were taking in the landscape of a Hera-sotern valley, close to the Village. Our love of the new terrain inspired us to undertake ventures on a regular basis. These short expeditions helped in the development of a registry for the identification of the strange fauna and flora of the planet. One whole year of progress placed us in a better position to analyze all the different properties of our new home.

One important discovery provided us with a clue to the greatest possible danger we might still face in the future—the Crustan threat. A visit from the Crustans, a species from a dimension beyond our universe called Crusta, represented a threat greater than any environmental aspect of the new planet. After our narrow escape from the conflict between the Andromeda and the three Crustan Warships, we always knew a time would come when we might face them again.

Because of the vast distances involved in deep space travel, the logistics of their return to our realm tended to be viewed more in terms of probability, than reality—but reality always finds a way of asserting itself. The location of a Crustan camp, with a spaceship launch platform found by one of our expeditions, remained uppermost in our minds.

Carla slid the research binoculars down over her eyes and squinted at the forest dwellers. The previous discovery of a dead specimen helped our researchers to ascertain much about these animals. The consequential information gathered placed us in a better position to determine the stages of an obvious evolutionary process, similar to the Earth's.

"They've sensed something—I don't think it's us—some other danger closer to them."

"Let me see." I pulled at the binoculars and she slipped the device off her head.

At a distance of five-hundred yards they appeared as large as life in the instrument and the details of age, temperature, height and weight appeared on the HUD.

"The larger male is the father and the slimmer, shorter one is the mother. They appear well-fed and the babies are twins—at a guess, about two years old. They do seem to be concerned about something," I said.

The male stood erect like a human. His height would reach to my shoulder but the broad, muscular chest and huge, ape-like arms indicated great agility and strength. Sparse contact with these beings still shrouded our knowledge of their habits and living conditions. We lacked an account of their history and our best research indicated their habitat to be more in trees than on the ground. The head of our resident paleontologist group and collator of all the study material on fauna and flora suggested the forest dwellers resembled the Earth's earlier hominins.

"Contact with them is so rare. I see the male appears to have a stick which looks a bit like a club —that's a first," said Carla. "Can I please have another look, hon?"

I passed the binoculars to her and she donned the instrument again and for a moment I watched her make the adjustments for a better view. I could not help notice the smile on her lips and the long blonde hair which flowed from beneath the protective cap she wore on her head. My unbridled infatuation with my wife's beautiful face and body never faltered at any time. To me she remained the loveliest of all creatures and whenever opportunity arose for me to gaze into her emerald-green eyes I would take it at length. With a sudden change of attitude the smile vanished from her lips.

"Oh, shoot! There's something in the bush adjacent to where they're positioned—I think it's one of those flying-hyena things."

I peered through the grass to see the object of her concern. Whatever lurked in the bush caught the attention of the family and the male took charge of his children with excited gesticulations and shouts. Carla's flying hyena had already been given the name—Dinabird. It did give one the impression of a hyena with wings—large wings, which folded close to its body. The creature weighed as much as a large dog and it hunted other animals for their flesh.

"The forest dweller is standing his ground and the children are scurrying off into the forest. This is going to be interesting, hon—we've never seen how these creatures react when threatened."

"Are you recording it," I asked.

"Of course. What do you think?"

The forest dweller stood erect to his full height and brandished the club in the face of the predator. The dinabird fluttered down from the branch of the tree, to land a few yards from its prey and with slow, precise steps, made its approach. Four, short, muscular legs supported the long body. The wings, which spanned out at least twenty feet, fluttered outward in an act of intimidation, to give the impression of size and strength. The forest dweller stood his ground and raised the club to head height in an attempt to scare the beast away but it continued to advance.

"That vicious thing will tear him to pieces," muttered Carla.

"You must leave it be, sweetheart. It's the way of all jungles and we shouldn't interfere."

"I know, but the forest dweller is so much like we are and has a family to provide for. I would hate to see that beast devour him. What would his family do?"

"Leave it, hon—don't unsettle yourself. I'm sure the forest dweller has a trick or two, up its sleeve."

We watched the face-off with interest and concern as the dinabird made a sudden lunge at the forest dweller. He took a quick step back and brought the club down on its back. The beast hesitated and shrugged off the blow. It remained in a crouch with wings held high and lunged forward to grasp the forest dweller on the leg, in its powerful jaws.

The club came down again, several times in quick succession. Our vision became obstructed by a cloud of red dust and we struggled to follow the action. The dinabird's wings flapped in frenzied frustration, accompanied by loud angry shrieks, to which the forest dweller gave vent to short grunts of determination, much like an agitated chimpanzee. The scuffle ended with a loud bellow from the dinabird and a screech of pain from the forest dweller. When the dust settled, neither of the combatants appeared to be upright. The sound of labored breath and guttural noises, emanated from the grass as we stood to our feet for a better view. Both creatures appeared to be incapacitated.

"Let's go and see—this is the first time we've ever witnessed a confrontation between these animals," I said.

We moved forward in a crouch and within a few minutes came across the battle scene. Carla, bless her heart, uttered words of sympathy for the forest dweller. He lay on his back with a gaping wound in one leg. The blood, a dark red, frothed from another wound in his chest. I checked on the dinabird which lay a few yards away but it showed no sign of movement. I nudged at it with my foot and the hyena-shaped head, flopped to one side and revealed a crushed cranium. The club had found its mark with a death-blow. I turned to see Carla on her knees with hand extended, about to touch the forest dweller's brow.

"Don't touch it, sweetheart—it's still alive."

My words fell on deaf ears. The creature's eyes fluttered open and gazed at her in amazement. The forest dweller, in obvious shock, did not react to the touch of her hand but held her gaze. I believed it knew we were there to help. The leg wound oozed blood and if the outflow could not be stemmed the creature stood little chance of survival. I knelt down beside Carla and with gentleness turned the head, which revealed another bad injury. The glazed eyes closed, as if in resignation of its fate.

"Hand me your first aid kit," demanded Carla.

"What are you going to do, sweetheart?"

"I'm going to see if I can save its life."

"Is that a wise thing?"

She glared at me. "We can't just allow it to die, Beckett. This creature is as close to a human being you will find on this planet—beside us, of course."

I have learned over the years never to argue with my wife when she gets that look on her face.

I plucked the small pouch off my belt and handed it to her. After a few minutes the forest dweller breathed easier and the eyes fluttered open again. We positioned ourselves to allow it, if driven by fear, to escape or the moment became too much for it, but my assessment of its wounds suggested otherwise.

The eyes sparkled in the sunlight as it stared into Carla's and some squeaky sounds came from its throat.

"Do you think it will live?" I asked.

"I have administered a nano-cure-all injection and rubbed healant into the wounds—I don't know."

A rustle in the foliage caused us to glance up. I turned my head to see the female forest dweller with the two children. They huddled together and observed us with fear in their eyes.

"I think they're intrigued by us," said Carla.

I stood with slow deliberation, to avoid movements which might be taken as a threat. The family cowered and took a step back but did not run away. I think they somehow knew we would not harm them.

"Let's step back a few paces sweetheart and allow them access," I said.

We moved away from the injured forest dweller and knelt down to pose less of a threat. A moment later the female came forward to where her mate lay, while the twins stayed in the background. They appeared to possess a system of communication and the female stretched out her hand to touch the male with a hesitant tenderness. She uttered low guttural sounds. The male still alive, did not seem able to respond and I felt by the female's expression, she understood him to be at the point of death. We waited while she continued to utter sounds of apparent comfort. I saw tears brim in the corner of her eyes—they appeared so human-like.

"I'm going to try and move closer," said Carla.

"Be careful, honey. We know nothing about these creatures."

"The female doesn't look concerned at our presence."

My hand rested on the hand-laser, hitched to my left side.

Carla moved with slow deliberation. She paused each time the female looked up at her. I could sense the creature's fear but it made no attempt to protect the injured forest dweller, or flee. The twins remained huddled together in the background, their eyes as large as saucers. It took Carla about two minutes to get close enough to touch the injured creature. The female tolerated her approach with small signs of apprehension but made no attempt to prevent Carla's presence. Perhaps it recognized the similarity of our bipedal structure and assumed us not to be hostile. After another few minutes Carla touched the injured forest dweller on the forehead and brought out a cloth from the emergency kit, to wipe its brow.

The male revived enough to open his eyes and with a shaky hand reached out to touch his partner's cheek with the back of his fingers—a gesture so human-like it astounded me. The female grabbed the hand and held it in her own. I waited to see what would transpire. Carla, emboldened by her own sense of intuition, placed her hand at the base of the male's neck and lifted the head. She removed a small flask of water from the kit and placed the neck onto its bottom lip. Water dribbled into the injured creature's mouth and it took a gulp. The female watched as Carla decanted the entire contents of the flask and mopped the perspiration from the forest dweller's brow.

I looked on in fascination. Both the forest dwellers appeared to grasp our desire to help them. Ten minutes later the male sat up by himself to view his mate with a look of affection. She stuck out her hand to stroke his head and with a sudden epiphany I believed these creatures to be as sentient as humans. They may not have the same intellectual capacity but possessed a primitive form of it. Another few minutes passed and the male tried to stand on its feet.

The female grasped her mate's arm and Carla stood to lend support and they raised him onto the one good leg. The healant Carla had poured into the wounds contained a nano-base of human DNA which repaired damaged tissue and cells. With the blood from the forest dwellers leg and chest wounds now stemmed, he showed the promise of a recovery.

The female indicated for us to move through the trees in a certain direction and I followed on behind while Carla helped her support the injured male. The children scampered around us, still on all fours but as fast as monkeys. Their interest in Carla knew no bounds. One youngster grabbed the leg of my coverall, stood upright and looked into my eyes—it appeared to be a young female. I guessed they did not see us as a threat.

A sudden movement in the branches above Carla caught my attention and I glanced up to see two large eyes amongst the leaves. The possibility of a second dinabird, perhaps the mate of the dead one, crossed my mind and I snatched the laser off my belt. The leaves parted and a bird as large as the first one, fluttered down in front of Carla and the two forest dwellers. It reared up with a shriek of anger and crept forward, toward us with jaws open and wings spread out wide. Carla stopped in her tracks and stared at the beast. I didn't wait but fired off a single shot into the creature's chest which stopped its forward momentum. My laser, set in stun mode did not incapacitate the dinabird. With another shriek of anger it further unfurled the giant wings and took off into the air. The forest dwellers stared at me and the laser in my hand. No doubt they thought I possessed some sort of magical power. We continued on until I could see a clearing up ahead. The forest trees around us extended to heights of about three hundred feet or more, and long vines from higher branches, hung down to the ground in many places.

All of a sudden we became surrounded by the brown furry creatures. I observed them slide down the vines from the canopy with the ease of apes, to surround us. Several of the number, males by their size, held clubs similar to the one our injured forest dweller had used. Four of them approached us in a threatening manner.

∞∞

TWO

Meeting the Clan

Carla stopped in her tracks. She released her grip on the injured forest dweller but as he started to fall she grabbed the arm again and gently eased him to the ground with the help of the female. I got ready to intervene but the female preempted me. She stood between Carla and the group. A cacophony of chatter, punctuated by snorts and shrieks rose from amongst the group and one of the males raised his club, to point it in our direction

The female screeched several syllables in an exchange of communication. After a standoff the male backed up to allow several of the females to come forward and inspect the injured forest dweller, while Carla stepped back to stand at my side. My hand rested on the butt of the laser as we waited for the group's further response to our presence.

"I don't think they want to harm us," said Carla.

"I'm not so sure about the large male. He made some hostile gestures in our direction."

"Give it time, hon. The female knows we have helped her. Imagine if we can gain the confidence of these creatures."

"They're definitely like the ancient hominins of our home planet. Hera-soter could be about three million years behind Earth, in its evolution. You'll remember they discovered the bones of a hominin on the continent of ancient Africa—a female they called, Lucy."

The group of females came closer and extended hesitant hands to touch us. The female kept an eye on the bigger males in the background. She warded off several youngsters who seemed fascinated by Carla's long blonde hair. I flinched as one of them touched my butt and the female gave a loud grunt to shoo the youngster away.

"Lucy seems very protective of us suddenly," I said.

Carla stroked the head of one tiny Forest dweller that clung to her leg and Lucy's eyes lit up. She chattered away to Carla in what appeared to be a conversational tone. We needed to find some way to establish a communication with her.

Two males came to help our injured forest dweller and we marveled at the care and gentleness with which they treated him. They easily lifted him and climbed the vines in the process. Lucy grabbed Carla's hand and pulled her forward in an attempt to lead us. Carla looked amused and with reluctance acquiesced to the creature's obvious suggestion. The group followed on behind and we progressed to the trunk of a large tree, where she stopped and pointed upward.

"I think she wants us to climb into this tree, hon," said Carla.

Several vines hung like ropes to the ground. I looked upward but the sheer density of leaves hid any potential destination.

"This might be a problem," I said.

Carla grabbed one of the vines and pointed to several growths, which appeared at various intervals. "These are much like ropes with knots tied into them. I think we should climb up as far as we can. I would love to see how they live."

I took one of the vines in hand. "My tree-climbing skills have never been great but I guess we can give it a go. They seem quite friendly now."

We pulled ourselves up on the vines and felt the extra weight of our bodies due to the higher gravity. Lucy took a vine beside us and climbed without any effort at all. She kept an eye and, on occasion waited, for us to catch up. It took about twenty minutes of strenuous effort to arrive at what appeared to be a constructed platform, onto which we both sprawled and I looked around in amazement. These people were more advanced than I gave them credit for. The construction involved beams lashed together with vines and by the thickness of the branches upon which our platform rested I assessed our height off the ground, to be over one hundred feet. The platform extended to boardwalks which appeared to go off in different directions—a classic type of tree-house.

Carla marveled at the construction as Lucy motioned us toward a doorway of what appeared to be a room, built from timber. We entered it to find a living area of about four square meters with a roof, which sloped upward to the main trunk. The forest dwellers were about five feet tall on average and we stooped down to enter. The low ceiling did not afford us the comfort of our full height. A whole new world opened for us and I could not wait to tell the others back at the village about it. I still carried the binoculars, which contained a video application for use in the field and took a few shots of the platform and the inside of the hut. A rough bench of vine-lashed timber hugged the walls and skins of animals lay strewn on the floor. In one corner the remains of an animal, which attracted a myriad of small insects, hung from the roof. With no signs of a place to cook I concluded fire had not yet made an appearance.

In the other corner, on several thick animal furs, lay our injured forest dweller. I could see by the pallor of his skin and the way he sat up when we entered, recovery would be imminent.

Carla put her arm around my waist. "Looks like we've been invited for dinner."

"I hope it's going to be that fruit in the corner and not the raw meat."

"It won't harm us to try— am just so fascinated by them. We have it within our power to advance their standards a thousand fold."

"I'm not sure such an advance would be good for them," I said.

"Well, first things first. We need to establish a means of communication."

"I doubt whether Ozzy's translator would help us either since the Lumbrians probably don't even have a clue these creatures exist."

Carla moved to the injured forest dweller's bedside and knelt down. He stared at her with large brown eyes and I imagined he might see her as some sort of god. Lucy came and knelt down beside the bed and extended both arms to embrace her mate. Tears flowed down her cheeks and they held each other for several moments. It appeared their lifestyle included a strong family relationship, with evidence of the pivotal emotion of love, at its nucleus.

Carla placed her hand on the injured forest dweller's arm and he reciprocated by placing his hand on her wrist in an action of gratitude. The twins, with remarkable discipline, watched us from the bench opposite and seemed to be in a constant attitude of awe. Lucy stood and walked to the corner, where several types of wild fruit nestled on small, bright colored stones. She picked out two of the same kind, which looked similar to an apple and offered one to Carla first who took a tentative bite into the flesh, to sample it.

She smiled at the forest dweller in acceptance of the gift. "That's really good."

Mine followed and I bit off a chunk. A strong and delightful aroma permeated the room as the sweet taste of the fruit's flesh titivated my taste buds. Lucy and her mate did not eat with us but watched with a contented satisfaction until we both devoured the fruit.

"This is wonderful stuff. I wonder where they found it—I haven't tasted anything so sweet on the planet so far."

Carla laughed. "I think we've just discovered a new delicacy and I'm sure, in time, they'll show us where to find it."

"I guess I know what you are going to be doing in the future. Perhaps we can trade some basic skills for knowledge of resources."

"I think this is a wonderful challenge for Laura," said Carla.

Laura Samuels, one of our crew members aboard the Andromeda and survivor of a fire in the ship's propulsion room, had asked Carla about involvement on our research and exploration team. After the death of her husband in the same fire, which almost cost us the mission she became involved with my ex executive officer, Gary Pearson, who turned out to be a traitor to our cause. Laura denied any collusion with Pearson and we couldn't prove otherwise. She held me responsible for her husband's death in the propulsion room fire. I gave the order to remove the breathable air in the room and flood it with an inert gas. The fire almost destroyed the ship but my quick action to save us all placed her and three other techs, in jeopardy. Gary Pearson, under incarceration in one of the escape pods met his end when the Crustans attacked the Andromeda.

"I agree, sweetheart. At least she speaks to you—she has not spoken to me since her husband died in the fire incident," I said.

"She needs something like this and who knows? It may bring her out of mourning."

"We can talk about it when we get back to base. I think we should be going—it'll be dark soon," I said.

We stood and Carla made a gesture with her hand that we would be leaving. I marveled at her ingenious sign language. First, to show we needed to climb down the tree trunk followed by a walking action, after which she placed both hands over her head to convey the meaning of a roof—our home.

Lucy watched with interest but made no sign she understood. Her mate, however, chirped and chortled a message to her and I gathered he understood to a degree what we intended. She turned and gathered up some fruit in her arms and handed them to us. I smiled and placed them in the chest-pocket of my coveralls as did Carla. I knelt down beside the injured forest dweller and touched his wrist. He in turn touched mine and we both understood it to be a goodbye.

We turned and left the hut to climb down the vines. Lucy and her children did not follow us but stood on the platform and stared after us with sad eyes. It dawned on me our meeting would not have been the first time we had been seen by them. The arrival of the escape pods must have produced a commotion in their treetop community. It is, however, a testimony to their stealth we seldom ever saw them. Most of their time would be spent in the trees, the foliage of which appeared so thick, as to make their homes invisible to us.

Back on the ground we moved off through the bushes toward the Village.

"Do we have a story to tell, or what?" I asked.

Carla glanced at me as we trudged along through the red, ankle-high grass.

"We not only have a story but we have a mission to plan—how we will bring these creatures into civilization."

∞∞

THREE

Alien Arrival

I turned to look at Lieutenant Sparkle. "Are you sure?"

'There is positive evidence of an arrival, Mr. Chairman.'

The android returned my stare with his two artificial blue orbs.

"Orbiting Hera-soter?"

'In a high orbit, Mr. Chairman—the observatory put it at one million kilometers.'

"Too far for the naked eye to see. They must know we're here."

The android shifted his position so I would not have to crane my neck.

'Without a doubt, sir. I think they are checking us out—assessing our strength. It will be interesting to see if they make a foray to their old base at Abrams Lake.'

The lake, named after Dr. Abrams, head of the Earth Relocation Project, rested at the base of an ancient volcano about fifty kilometers from the Village.

"I have dreaded this day," I said.

'We all knew it would come, sir.'

"Call the entire village together in the quadrangle. It's best to let everyone know what's happening."

'Yes, sir. I notice Mrs. Samuels has a class of forest dwellers in the lecture hall. Do you want me to have them sent home?'

"I think it'll be okay for the time being, Sparkle. The locals are very much a part of our family here. You may ask if one of them can take a message to Charley. I think it would be good for him to hear what I have to say. We'll meet in one hour."

Sparkle turned and left me to ponder our fate. The Crustans would never consider peace. Their warlike nature made the extension of an olive branch impossible. Besides, we destroyed three of their warships and they would not forget. Ozzy, our alien friend from the Lumbrian dimension, reassured us of this fact. Trans-Lumbrian attempts at peace ended in Crustan disregard for signed treaties, of which there had been several dozen over a million years of conflict. According to Ozzy, our space-time stemmed from the propagation of a process the Lumbrians called, seeding. This reality escapes my comprehension to this day.

I left my office to find Carla. She would be either in the lab with my valet, Happydoo, or in the canteen with a mug of caffeen. I found her in the latter.

"Not researching flora and fauna today, sweetheart?"

"I was but Happydoo decided to get himself charged up."

I sat down opposite her and leaned back in the chair. "I have some bad news."

She sat up straight. "Has someone been injured?"

"No—much worse I'm afraid. A Crustan vessel has been detected in high orbit."

"Oh, God, no—is it a warship?"

"We can't tell yet but I am pretty sure it is."

"What are we going to do, Beckett?"

"Keep it under observation for now. If they make any aggressive moves we will implement the first phase of the plan."

"Are you going to tell everyone?"

"Yes—I'm holding a meeting in the quadrangle one hour from now."

"What about the forest dwellers?"

"I have sent for Charley. You may check to see if Lucy is in Laura's class. She should attend."

Charlie and Lucy's progress, from their original status to the present, could be described as dynamic. Our comparison to the hominin status of ancient Earth did little justice to their intellectual capabilities. I did notice their frontal lobes protruded more than Earth's typical transitional creatures and it is possible they resemble the first homo-sapiens in basic intellect. In two years their grasp of our language advanced from zero to basic sentences, with a limited vocab. To Carla and I, they seemed more like pets than colleagues but as their intellectual prowess increased, our relationship changed with it.

"I have spoken to Lucy several times about the Crustans and she understands them to be our enemies. She told me of their first sighting of the aliens—they understood the risks of exposure," said Carla.

"So, the Crustans don't even know they exist?"

"I shouldn't think so. The alien base at Abrams Lake serves as a stop-off point for their prospectors. According to Lucy they never saw the Crustans in the forests or anywhere other than at the lake. The lake would suit their semi-aquatic requirements."

"They will have seen the Andromeda in orbit so they will know we're here," I said.

Carla placed her mug on the table. "I see the people are gathering in the quad."

"Let's go tell them the bad news."

We left the canteen and walked hand in hand to the central village area and stood in front of the command pod. Laura Samuels and her forest dwellers stood at the back of the crowd, all eager to hear the news

"Thank you for all coming at such short notice. I have been informed that the alien species which attacked our spaceship on route to Herasoter, have recently arrived in a high orbit. There is no need to panic. We will implement the plan at the sound of the horn. Take only the things you need for emergency purposes and make your way to the designated safe-places. We have no idea what the aliens will do, so I ask you to go about your normal business, until you hear the signal. All forays out into the forests are now prohibited. I ask for the committee members to meet with me in the command pod."

The people stood and chatted for several moments before drifting off, back to their various activities. The entire group had lived in anticipation of this day's arrival and knew the roles they needed to play.

One by one, the committee members ambled into the command pod and seated themselves to await a short recap of the plan. The members represented the different sections of our group. The two androids, Lieutenant Sparkle and Happydoo, completed the council of twenty-four, who directed the process of the colony's wellbeing and growth in the areas of Agriculture, Business, Industry, Medical, Education and all the Sciences.

Carla retained the security portfolio and Lieutenant Sparkle provided a Military presence. Happydoo in conjunction with Mickey, our Master

Computer, acted as administrator and keeper of records.

"Everyone knows exactly what they are responsible for and what immediate actions need to be taken. I suggest we start by removing important stuff to the various safe-places. We need to make sure there'll be a sufficient amount of food and water available if a siege takes place."

Lieutenant Sparkle raised a hand. 'We need Ozzy's help in removing the final aspects of our anti-matter gun from the Andromeda, Sir.'

"I will be onto that shortly, Sparkle. Are there any other questions?"

The plan, devised over a period of time, came up on every meeting's agenda but, with the arrival of the aliens, the subject now took on a greater urgency.

I turned to Herbert Matheson, our Technology representative. "Are we able to view the complete orbit of the enemy craft?"

"Yes, Mr. Chairman. Our observatory stations are all in operation and the enemy's heat signature is being tracked around the clock. Each station will keep CCT contact with Lieutenant Sparkle so we'll know when the enemy makes its move."

I turned to Happydoo. "Make sure you contact me immediately if there's any change in the warship's position."

'I am happy to do that for you, Master Beckett.'

The meeting ended and everyone went off in different directions. I felt a measure of trepidation despite all our plans and suspected there would be more enemy arrivals. The Crustans understood we possessed a formidable weapon—technology a little more advanced than their own—compliments of our alien universal overseer, Ozzy, the antimatter cannon had saved our skins on the Andromeda's first confrontation with the enemy.

Carla and I decided to go home and check over our emergency survival kits when Charley, with Lucy in hand, arrived. The two forest dwellers had become attached to us after the dinabird episode. Charley crouched in front of me with his head bowed in respect and Lucy hung back at the entrance. My greeting would always be to touch the top of his head and he would respond with great exuberance in the form of a bear hug. The forest dwellers picked up our human habits with the enthusiasm of little children and merged these with their own.

"Charlee him greet Charmin Buckitt."

I greet you too Charlie—how are you today?"

"Charlee, him good, Charman Buckitt."

For some reason related to phonetics the forest dwellers struggled with certain sounds and my first name became pronounced as 'Buckitt', instead of Beckett.

"Did Lucy tell you about the shalumpah?" I asked.

The shalumpah, a word translated from their language, indicated the Crustans.

"Yus, yus Mastah Buckitt—bad shalumpah him come. All Bashuku must hide."

The Bashuku referred to the forest dwellers, of which there appeared to be only one species. We asked Charley if any other of his kind existed on the continent but he didn't know. It would appear the Bashuku did not rove far from their habitat.

Charlie understood the threat posed by the aliens. The forest Dwellers witnessed many atrocious animal kills on the edge of the forest close to the lake, before the Crustans left. The Bashuku killed only to feed themselves. They retained a huge respect for their surroundings whereas the Crustans destroyed both flora and fauna for fun. I doubted whether Charley understood our plans to defend everyone but he told me he would allow us to use the tree resorts as a final hideaway if our safe-places became compromised by the enemy.

The two forest dwellers left us after a short discussion about their family. We also talked about the areas where a type of long-horned, shaggy-haired buffalo called Barakis, could be hunted. The Bashuku were excellent hunters and often provided us with gifts of barakis meat.

"I really hope the Crustans never discover the forest dwellers," said Carla.

I agreed and added my own thoughts. "We must never be the reason such a discovery is made."

"I must call up Ozzy on the emergency transmitter. We need to move on the final deconstruction of the antimatter weapon on the Andromeda and transfer it to the planet."

We left the command pod and walked to our home, a rough two bedroom, timber abode, not far from the main quadrangle of the village. I found the emergency transmitter and activated a distress call to Ozzy. No matter what his location the signal would find him. He always treated my calls with urgency—the last time I used it had been after our arrival in the orbit of our new planet. Due to the damaged EEP's, Lieutenant Sparkle and I had no other way to transcend to the planet's surface but to ask our alien friend for help.

"Now all we can do is wait. He'll know this involves the Crustans so it should not be long before we see him."

She came into the room with two mugs of cafteen and set them down on the table.

"At least we'll be able to get the anti-matter weapon finalized and working on Hera-soter's soil. Where are you going to situate it, hon?"

"Lieutenant Sparkle feels the correct place will be high up on one of the mountain range peaks. We have several possible venues."

"So, the plan is to use the force-field from the Andromeda to protect the command pod area?"

"That's the plan, sweetheart. I think the first indication of an attack might be the destruction of the Andromeda. It's unfortunate but we can't protect it without the barrier but it's more important to shield the command pod from attack."

"Yes, it is a pity. I would love to have conducted future tours when the new arrivals make their debut," she replied.

"I'm sure the future spaceships from Earth will be more versatile than the Andromeda. They'll be able to land on the planet."

"I can't wait for the second group to arrive—I miss your dad and Freda," said Carla.

"Likewise, but it will be sometime before they get here. We have to hope and pray we can overcome the Crustan threat first."

"Do you think Ozzy will be able to convince his superiors Hera-soter is worth saving? I know he has tried several times but they keep telling him to get on with his oversight of the universe."

"I believe the war between the Lumbrians and the Crustans is reaching a stage where all their resources will be fully extended. If the Crustans move their forces into our universe on a greater scale they will have no option but to follow."

"Is that a good or a bad thing," asked Carla.

"Equally, both. It will be good for us because the local Crustan forces will be caught up in the war and attention should be drawn away from us. It'll be bad for the universe because all the resident species will be drawn into the conflict."

"Let's hope that never happens."

A sudden knock on the door interrupted our dialogue. I walked into our sitting room and found Happydoo at the door.

"What's up, Happydoo?"

'Its not good news, unfortunately Master Beckett. We have received a report—there are now five Crustan ships in the same orbit as the first. They are gathering a significant force.'

∞∞

FOUR

The Antimatter Cannon

Five days later Ozzy made his appearance. The Orbitron landed on the quadrangle beside the command pod. The jubilant alien greeted us with enthusiasm.

"Greetings Earthlings. Carla, my dear, Beckett, dear boy—how great to see the two of you again."

The sight of Ozzy would have a stranger in hysterics. His long tubular, condom-shaped body with its four stubby arms and no legs, made him appear as a character from a science fiction comic strip. He floated along, about twelve inches off the ground and farted out air from diaphragms on the side of his head. One large eye occupied the space above a slit, which served as a mouth. In the Lumbrian dimension a different breathable medium fed their cardo-vascular system but Ozzy, fitted with some type of transforming device breathed the Hera-sotern air without any problem. The most disturbing aspect of his aesthetic appearance rested in a transparency of skin, through which shapes of internal organs could be seen. It took some getting used to.

We brought Ozzy into our home and he looked around with admiration.

"Well done. Not as luxurious as your digs on the Andromeda but certainly comfortable."

The alien's visits always provided us with new information about the other resident species, too numerous to mention in the Universe. We sat and chatted for an hour before Ozzy returned to the Orbitron where he spent the night. Carla and I turned in and tried to settle our thoughts.

In the morning I called Lieutenant Sparkle and we discussed the removal of the antimatter equipment from the Andromeda. Herbert Matheson joined us and after an hour of intense planning I called for Carla and Happydoo. Ozzy outlined a plan as to how we would transport the parts. The limited space within the Orbitron restricted the operation and Ozzy concluded that three trips would be required to complete the move.

I asked him if the Crustans might have observed his approach to the planet.

"No chance, dear boy. The Orbitron possesses a stealth mode the enemy does not have. It gives us an advantage over them."

*

Later in the day we arrived at the entrance hatch of the Andromeda. I contacted the Andromeda's orbit computer for permission to come aboard and received a terse answer to proceed. Mickey, the Andromeda's Master Control processor now resided in the command pod, on Herasoter. Ozzy guided the Orbitron through the open bay doors of the entry dock and parked in the main warehouse area. When pressure and air stabilized we clambered out onto the familiar deck of the ship.

Lieutenant Sparkle and Matheson went straight to the antimatter turrets to retrieve the remnant of equipment while Ozzy and I took the verticap to the bridge. As a matter of protocol I made the relevant entry of our visit in the President Commander's log. The orbit computer did not engage in conversation as Mickey did—its program allowed brief commands and short answers to questions with the sole purpose of the ship's orbital requirements.

I knew the occasion might be my last visit to the Andromeda. The Crustans would destroy it at the first opportunity. At a guess, the enemy might be holding off on an attack, to spy on us and see what they could glean with their long range visual equipment. We could assume they might also be waiting for more reinforcements, after which an attack on the village could be expected.

The Andromeda's protective shield, another piece of equipment previously removed from the Andromeda, would provide some protection. A bunker with an auxiliary console, from which we could operate the antimatter cannon, had been built beneath the command pod. If the Crustans discovered the weapon site on the mountain peak, we might be in trouble from there on. When the cannon is fired there is no visible beam to draw the enemy's attention but with heat-seeking equipment they might be able to pin-point its location.

With the last of the antimatter equipment deposited on Hera-soter, Ozzy returned to the Andromeda and the time had come to say a final farewell to my old command. I took the time to glance around the bridge—for me it represented almost sixty years of service. A multitude of memories overwhelmed my reflection and I forced myself to break away from the scene and move toward the verticap. Several moments later I squashed into the Orbitron with the others. Ozzy's single eye held mine in a brief gaze of sympathy. He knew my emotions would be on a knife's edge.

"Don't worry, dear boy. They may not destroy it and once they have left the universe we can return and make it into the museum you and Carla so ardently desire."

I gave him a wistful look. "That would be too much to hope for my alien friend but it's a great thought."

Without further incident we journeyed back to the planet's surface and offloaded the remainder of our load.

*

The two barakis, courtesy of Charley and Lucy's small herd of tame, long-horned Buffalo-like animals, carried the antimatter cannon's stubby barrel and the priming system, on their backs. The heavy load, in conjunction with the mountain's terrain, caused the beasts much discomfort and displeasure. They shrieked and made guttural snorts at every opportunity. At one point, on a steep portion of the incline they sat back on their haunches and wailed.

The forest dwellers maintained the barakis mainly for a substance similar to milk, which the beasts produced from their udders, much like the cows on Earth. The animals also provided a constant supply of meat. Beside one forest dweller our party consisted of Happydoo, Chief Spanner, Herbert Matheson and I. We all did our best to encourage the beasts with shouts and slaps on their rumps.

The weight would have been too great for us to carry for such a distance and although we felt sorry for the animals there appeared to be no other way forward. I could have had Ozzy deliver the weapon straight from the Andromeda to the site but at the time a suitable place had not been found. Unfortunately our alien friend could not spare any more time with us. The war in the Lumbrian dimension required his earnest attention and his superiors demanded his return. All the other related equipment for the establishment of a turret and accommodation of the weapon had been moved on the alien's previous visits.

One of Charley's tribe scouted out an appropriate site on the mountain top plus a manageable route which would not be too tough for the barakis. The slopes posed little problem but further up, the cliffs towered above our entourage. The forest dweller, one of Charley's brothers, guided us between large boulders and through crevices, which often threatened to have the entire train cast into the valley below.

Herbert Matheson, not the fittest of people, stopped to wipe his brow. "How much further does this terrible terrain go?"

"For at least another hundred yards before it opens up for the final push to the top," I said.

The two androids enjoyed far better climbing ability and offered their assistance to Herbert us, in our struggles. Chief Spanner led the two barakis up front and pulled on their vine straps to encourage continued forward progress. Happydoo brought up the rear with his usual techno-humor insults at my lack of dexterity, followed by my occasional mutters. Twice, when I lost my footing and slipped, he grabbed me by the shoulders and lifted me back onto the path. His pirouette and foot-stomp routine would follow my grateful remarks.

Later in the afternoon we broke through the difficult terrain and encountered an almost level area which led toward the final peak. I decide we all needed a rest and stopped the procession, to sit on a group of rocks, while the barakis munched away at the red-colored grass. A few minutes later I walked to a ledge which overlooked the forests below. The view stretched out to the shore of Abram's Lake in the distance and I could see the Village far below us. The shrill shrieks of the two barakis interrupted my reverie and I turned to see Chief Spanner provoking them to get on the move again. The sun would be down within two hours and we needed to make the peak of the mountain before darkness fell.

A greater concern warranted our attention, however—a sudden turn in the weather conditions. Heavy clouds hovered overhead, filled with rain and possible hail. Hera-soter's rain came in two of its seasons. We called them seasons but they differed from Earth's four seasons. The coldest season came over the mid-year, in the twenty-fifth week, and brought the heaviest rainfalls. Around the fiftieth week, the weather brought a light misty rain in the evenings to balance out the heat of the summer days. In between, the conditions remained mild and the morning sunrise dispersed a soft mist, which gathered again in the late afternoons.

The final assault on the peak lay before us and we hastened onward to get to the rocky outcrop which would serve as the site. The rain came moments before the protection of the cliff could be gained and we all stumbled along in the downpour toward a protective overhead ledge. The huge drops of rain came down hard and despite the overhang no one escaped a thorough drenching. The barakis huddled as close to the cliff face as their loads would allow. Herbert Matheson and I did our best to crouch behind the baraki while the forest dweller curled up into ball beneath one of the barakis.

The two androids stood out in the rain, impervious to the water, and waited. It took a full hour before the downpour subsided and we continued on our way. The forest dweller led us around the cliff face to a steep incline of hard soil, a natural pathway between several large boulders and we all crowded behind the barakis, to push them up the incline. With a final effort we made it to the top and I breathed a long sigh of relief. Darkness fell as we walked onto a natural, rocky shelf. This platform would serve as the site for our antimatter cannon.

The weapon's base construction, composed of four metal beams, secured to the rock floor by a special bonding compound which took a matter of minutes to set up. The rest could wait for the morning and Charley's brother tied the barakis up to a tree. We made ourselves comfortable for the long night ahead.

∞∞

FIVE

A Wrong Step

Chief Spanner and Herbert Matheson completed the installation of the weapon by mid-day. The weapon primed on immediate response to its activation and the test target, a large outcrop of rock on an adjacent peak, dissolved as the charged particles hit their mark. We wanted to avoid the mishap of the weapon's first deployment when it refused to prime, due to misalignment of the perimeter rods. This unfortunate circumstance gave the enemy an advantage until Lieutenant Sparkle's unexpected return.

"Are you sure the alignment problem won't happen again?"

Matheson's confidence gave me reason for hope. "The misalignment came as a result of extreme vibration caused by the enemy nukes. The only thing that will prevent the cannon from functioning is a direct hit on this facility."

"Does the distance the signal needs to travel, result in a delay?"

"There should be no detectable delays under distances of five-hundred miles. Mr. Chairman."

The arduous trek back down the mountain took longer than expected. The initial descent brought no mishaps until we came across a series of crags, strewn with loose boulders. The barakis bellowed and shrieked their uncertainty and it took all of Chief Spanner's ingenuity to coax the two animals down the slope.

A short plateau of level ground followed and ended with a ridge of rock, before the ground fell away. The previous evening's rain had made the path along the edge of the ridge, slippery and difficult to negotiate. On several occasions both Matheson and I needed the android's to help us. Charley's brother appeared unperturbed by the conditions, a legacy of many years of hunting on the same mountain slopes.

My descent took an unfortunate turn when I ventured too close to the ridge of the plateau and lost my footing. Happydoo lunged to grab my arm but slipped in the soft clay and the two of us tumbled down the steep slope. The android managed to grasp the branch of a bush but I continued over a low ridge, to land against a boulder, which prevented me from a fatal fall to the bottom of a ravine. A terrible pain engulfed my right leg and I passed out.

Happydoo arrived before anyone else. I'm not sure how long it took me to revive but when I did the android sat on its haunches and cradled my head.

'Master Beckett...Master Beckett, wake up.'

I opened my eyes and the pain immediately registered in my brain.

'Be still Master Beckett. You've broken your leg.'

I groaned and closed my eyes again. "I am so fucking stupid. How bad is it, Happydoo?"

The android looked down at the leg and its eyes pulsated. "It's bad Master Beckett.'

The others all arrived at the same time and gathered around.

"Oh shit, Beckett. You've done yourself a dis-service," said Matheson.

Chief spanner took over. As the chief technician in charge of maintenance aboard the Andromeda, medical aid for humans had been a necessity. He looked at my leg.

'You have a proximal tibia fracture. We'll have to make you a splint, Mr. Chairman. All we have in the way of medicine is a pain-killer and a tissue healant, which will at least keep the swelling down. It will also deal with any infection. Beyond that, there isn't much we can do but put you on one of the barakis.'

I managed to sit up and view the bottom half of my leg—the shin bone stuck out at an angle.

"Give me the pain-killer before you yank the leg straight," I said.

Chief Spanner opened a panel on his thigh and produced four capsules. 'This will only take about ninety seconds to work, Mr. Chairman. You won't feel much pain after that—don't worry.'

I swallowed the capsules. Within moments my body lost all feeling.

'Can I do it now, Mr. Chairman?'

I consented and the chief grabbed my leg before I could relent. I felt no pain at all—marvelous twenty-fourth century pain-killers. Without further ceremony the two android's loaded me onto the back of a barakis and Happydoo remained at my side to keep a hand on me for stability over the rough terrain. We toiled on down the slope and arrived at the base of the mountain without further incident.

"Carla's going to be mad at me for being so stupid," I said.

Happydoo gave me a quizzical glance. 'I should think she would be happy to see you back, all in one piece, Master Beckett—even if a measure of stupidity was involved.'

"You're a tin smart-ass, you bucket of rusting bolts."

The android burst into the foot-stomp routine. When he performed his pirouette I almost fell off the back of the barakis.

An hour later we trooped into the village and the barakis ceased their incessant bellows. Carla came out of the office with a smile but when she saw my leg, her face contorted in surprise.

"What have you done to yourself, hon?"

'Master Becket has broken his leg Mrs. Carla,' said Happydoo.

"I took a little tumble on the mountain, sweetheart. It's nothing."

"Nothing?" she shouted.

"The healing module is still up there in the Andromeda—you've got a broken leg and you say it's nothing?"

"It will heal on its own."

"Without the right equipment it will take six months to heal properly," she said. I could sense her exasperation, but what could I do.

"Let it go, babe. I'll be okay."

The two android's helped me off the back of the beast and set me down on the ground.

Carla's comment regarding the right equipment stung a little. It had been my decision to leave much of the medical apparatus on board the Andromeda. The convenience of Ozzy's Orbitron, I felt would be better served, with more of our comfort items—my mistake.

"Really, hon. This is a bad time—with the Crustans on our doorstep. What are we going to do with you?" "I'm sorry, my love but shit happens. We'll just have to deal with it. I'll get Chief spanner

51

to come up with up a wheel chair, or something similar, and Happydoo can push me around."

'I'd be happy to do that for you Master Beckett. I'll mention it to the Chief and he can get started right away.'

Happydoo lifted me with gentle care and walked to our home where he deposited me on the rough wooden settee. Carla followed to make me as comfortable as possible.

"Is there any change in the Crustan's position," I asked.

'Two more warships have attached themselves to the group, Master Beckett.'

"That makes seven ships altogether."

I decided to initiate the first part of our defense strategy—activation of the protective shield. If the Crustans attacked the village and scored a direct hit on the command pod, the shield would absorb much of the impact. The village homes, however, might all be destroyed. The people would need to escape to the safe-places in the mountain caves at the first sign of hostility.

"Call the committee together, Happydoo. They need to come immediately to our home. I also need one of our medical specialists to check my leg out when the meeting is over."

'I will be happy to initiate both your requests, Master Beckett'

*

After a short meeting with the Committee members the two androids remained to discuss a few possible scenarios.

"I think they are likely to destroy the Andromeda first and then bomb the village," I mused.

Lieutenant Sparkle entertained different thoughts.

'I don't think the Crustans would use a destructive device to destroy everything, sir. I think it quite likely they might try to intimidate us into capitulation first—if that failed, they would probably land a few of their craft and invade us with a combatant force.'

"You may be correct, Sparkle but if we use the antimatter gun it will motivate them to destroy us with the strongest weapons at their disposal."

'We can only wait and see what their first move is, sir.'

Happydoo's eyes pulsed with a sudden vigor and he cocked his head to one side.

'I am receiving an audio only, message from Mickey, Master Beckett. The message is coming from deep space.'

We all waited in anticipation but I had to ask the question.

"You did say it was a message from deep space and not the orbiting Warships?"

"It may be from a ship in transit from their dimensional entry point," said Carla.

'It appears not to be of Crustan origin, Mrs. Carla. The message is dated 2371 CE and emanates from a region near the Polaris Star.'

"What on Earth are you saying, Happydoo?"

Lieutenant Sparkle gave the answer. *'I believe it's a space vessel in transit from the planet Earth to Hera-soter, Mr. Chairman.'*

∞∞

SIX

The Second Earth Mission

"Oh my God—the second mission from Earth, already?" said Carla.

I turned to Happydoo. "Tell Mickey to relay the entire message when he has received it."

We all stared at each other. A transit vessel from Earth meant the Relocation Project to be many months ahead of schedule and the news came as a shock. The Crustan presence complicated matters and for a moment I experienced some regret at the timing of the new arrivals. It may, however, be fortuitous that the Earth Mission would arrive after the Crustans. I needed more information.

The Crustans might attack them before they could make a safe landing on Hera-soter—I might need to ask the ship commander if he could steer clear of the planet until the Crustan problem was resolved. They may arrive to find us all prisoners, or worse—dead.

The blue lights in Happydoo's eyes pulsated as he received the completed message from Mickey. I could see by his synthetic smile, the news pleased him. The android bobbed its head once and initiated the recording. A woman's voice spoke to us.

"Seeking contact with President Commander, Dr. Beckett Conroy of the pioneer vessel Andromeda. Date: 10th January, 2371 CE.

This is the galactic starship, Prime Endeavor—President Commander Cruse in command. We are in transit from Earth to the exoplanet 51 Peg d in the Constellation of Pegasus, with a total compliment of twenty-five hundred people. Our date of exit from Sol's system was on the 15th January, 2329 CE. We are travelling at seventy-five percent light speed and should soon enter the 51 Pegasi solar system. We are ahead of schedule and are approximately one Earth month from arrival on Hera-soter.

Please answer immediately with due consideration for time delay.

President Commander, Rebecca Cruse, out."

The complex calculation of an arrival date provided a challenge only AI could work out. A rough estimation of about thirty-six days popped into my mind which meant the fiasco of a Crustan attack on our planet would be historical by the time of the prime Endeavor's arrival.

"Prepare a message for the Prime Endeavor, Mickey. Tell President Commander Cruse about the potential Alien threat we're facing and the uncertainty of the outcome. Advise her, in the event of the demise, or capture of our colony, it would be wise to keep their distance, until the enemy leaves the area."

'I will transmit the message immediately, Mr. Chairman and keep them abreast of matters as time progresses.'

Carla raised her eyebrows. "President Commander Cruse is a woman—how compelling."

"Equal job, equal pay, sweetheart," I said.

"What are we going to do," asked Carla.

I gave it a moment's thought. "I'm not sure —but they need to know the truth regarding our present situation. We don't know how long the enemy will continue to orbit, or when they will attack."

Lieutenant Sparkle's eyes pulsed. 'It's possible the Crustans have picked up the transmission from the Prime Endeavor. If they know another ship is arriving from Earth it may prompt them to move sooner.'

One of our resident medical specialists arrived to attend to my leg. He carried a metal case which I assumed contained the necessary treatment and solutions for my damaged leg. He knelt down to inspect the wound. "Done yourself a mischief, Mr. Chairman?"

"Not the best prank I've played. What does it look like?"

"Whoever set the bone did a great job—you should live. The healant in our emergency medical packs are extremely efficient and the wound looks clean enough."

"Thanks to Chief Spanner," I said.

He removed the make-shift splint and applied a solvent around the wound to remove the congealed blood, then produced a spray canister. I marveled at the efficiency of the pain-killers.

The medic sprayed a foam substance over the area of the break. "This foam will solidify and act as a splint. It will also take care of any infection that tries to set in but I suggest you do not put any weight on the leg for at least three weeks."

This news did not sit well with me. Any amount of incapacitation constituted a restriction to my leadership. The healing module on the Andromeda would facilitate the knitting of the bone in a much shorter span of time but the ship remained out of our reach. Ozzy would more than likely not come back while the Crustan Warships still commanded Hera-sotern space.

The medic finished up and gave me some more pain-killers. "You'll start to feel pain in about two hours. Take one of these capsules and it should last ten hours. I will ask one of our medical technicians to print you a set of crutches—it's the best I can do for the moment."

"Thanks—I'm sure Mrs. Conroy will take good care of me."

"As if you would listen to any words of restriction," said Carla.

Happydoo interrupted. 'I will be happy to carry you anywhere you need to go, Master Beckett.'

"Thankyou Happydoo—we need to get back to more serious matters. As soon as I get my crutches I'll be able to move about a bit better and barring any emergency situation, should be able to do fine on my own."

"We need to get you to the auto-dress fabricator in the maintenance module. It will spin you a uniform to suit your encumbrance," said Carla.

One of the Andromeda's original escape pods contained the colony's sole auto-dress fabricator. Many of the folk chose to wear rough clothes, made from wild animal pelts and refrained from the nano-fabricator's use. Our industrialization of lifestyle refinements, such as clothes and furniture, progressed at a slow rate as there were many other issues to concentrate on. The raw materials, from which the dress-fabricators manufactured their tiny nano-particle fiber, required a certain amount of supplementation from the natural resources, which we still needed to find on our new home planet. No doubt, in time we would recover our original style of living and comfort, but for now we made do with old coveralls and whatever clothes the colony's burgeoning industry could produce.

*

Several days later I sat on a log, outside the main pod when Lieutenant Sparkle's digital purr interrupted my thoughts.

'There is a change taking place in the position of the warships in orbit, Mr. Chairman.'

I grabbed my crutches and clumped into the pod. Sparkle sat at the console in obvious consultation with Mickey, our master control computer.

"Speak to me, Mickey. What's happening."

'One of the Crustan warships has dropped out of orbit and is descending to the planet's surface, Mr. Chairman.'

"Is the barrier over the command pod one hundred percent activated?"

'It remains at maximum strength, Mr. Chairman.'

The colony's administrative area included the original escape pods, along with a few huts, which contained our main food and water storage for the village. The command pod contained a small nuclear, fission reactor which supplied the colony with power.

"I think it's time to get everyone to the safe places. Activate the siren, please, Mickey."

A wailing sound emanated from the command pod's roof and I could see people outside look up in shock as they comprehended the situation. The village emptied, except for Carla, Happydoo, Lieutenant Sparkle, Chief Spanner and I. The people all fled out toward the farm and to the base of the mountain where the caves were located. The energy barrier protecting us, radiated out from four vertical beams about thirty feet high and provided an overhead, protection span of about one thousand square feet. If a missile struck, the barrier would disperse the force outward, to the surrounding area and we would survive in the bunker beneath the pod.

"How long before the enemy craft is in range to fire?"

It's not moving at high velocity, Mr. Chairman. I estimate it will take about ten minutes to reach the edge of Hera-soter's atmosphere. They could fire a missile at any time.'

Carla entered the pod, her face a picture of concern. "What's happening, hon?"

"There's one enemy craft on its way to the planet. I've decided to evacuate the village."

Happydoo and Chief Spanner arrived in unison.

'Should we descend into the bunker, Master Beckett?'

"Yes—we can monitor their movement from there—let's go."

We all clambered down through a hatch into the bunker, via a wooden ladder. The bunker's walls, fortified by panels stripped from the outer-hull of the maintenance pod, would serve as some protection from a cave-in from shockwaves. The androids would be impervious to any radiation but Carla and I needed protection. We each donned an EVA suit, compliments of the Andromeda and took up positions at a workbench, which contained a holographic platform with an attached control panel.

I turned the system on. A holo, showing the position of six warships in geo-synchronous orbit, appeared on the platform. The seventh ship, now at the edge of the planet's atmosphere glowed red as it encountered the oxygen-rich air.

"They haven't fired on us yet," I said.

'I don't believe they will, Mr. Chairman. I think this is a recce mission to get a personal close-up view of things,' said Sparkle.

The craft swooped down toward the lake and over the vacant base used by the initial Crustan prospectors. We waited with trepidation to see the direction the craft would take and our fears heightened as it swung in an arc to fly directly over the village.

"They're being pretty bold," said Carla.

In a blink of an eye the warship shot over the village at a height of a thousand feet and disappeared into the blue, back into space. Carla and

I breathed a sigh of relief. We waited a few more moments to see if there would be any change in direction but the craft made straight for the orbiting fleet. After the removal of our EVA's, we turned off the holo-platform and climbed back to the pod above.

'Should we recall everyone to the village, Master Beckett?'

"Not yet. We don't know what the aliens will do next. That flyby wasn't because they are getting bored—an attack might still be imminent."

I turned to Lieutenant Sparkle. "Tell Mickey to drop the energy-barrier for now—there's no sense in wasting precious energy until we need it."

The distinct hum of the barrier disappeared and I clumped back to my log seat outside the pod, for a rest. The effort of getting around caused the pain in my leg to escalate and I popped another pain-killer. Carla stood behind me and rested her forearms on my shoulders.

"Are you okay, hon?"

"Yeah, I'm fine—just need another pain-killer." I leaned back against her breasts and cradled my head on her shoulder. Lieutenant Sparkle, his synthetic brow creased in rivulets of lines, came out of the pod.

'Sorry to worry you Mr. Chairman but there is another message from deep space.'

∞∞

SEVEN

The Alien Fleet makes a Move

I pulled myself up with help of a crutch and with Carla in tow, stumped back into the pod. A measure of trepidation, mixed with cautious excitement overtook me as I sat down at the console.

"Give it to me Mickey."

'Coming through clearly, Mr. Chairman.'

The holo-platform sprang to life—the head and shoulders of an attractive woman, with beautiful white hair and steel blue eyes, appeared. Commander Cruse's voice spoke through the speakers set in the ceiling above our heads.

"Greetings Mr. Chairman. Your message was received with much excitement on behalf of the Prime Endeavor's crew and secular compliment. It has been forty-two years in the making for us and we cannot wait to set foot on Herasotern soil. Your warning regarding the alien threat is taken with serious consideration of your plight. Our ship is an upgraded version of the Andromeda and we carry heavy armaments with the latest ordinance available compliments of

Earth's military. We are expecting your enemy to ping us soon as our vessel is now within the 51 Peg solar system. If they come to inspect us we will be prepared for a fight. I have instructed our Master Computer to set us in a three-billion kilometer orbit around Hera-soter until we hear from you again. Please send an update immediately on receipt of this message and repeat the action every day.

Commander Cruse, out."

Carla stared at the speakers intently for a few seconds. "What are we going to tell them, hon?"

"We'll tell them the enemy has made a recce of our village and surrounding area and we expect an attack will be imminent. We will keep them updated as much as the circumstances allow. Do you copy, Mickey?"

'Loud and clear, Mr. Chairman. I will send the answer to Commander Cruse immediately.'

"The time delay will become minimal at three billion kilometers and we will soon be able to have an actual conversation with them." I said.

'The enemy warship has rejoined the others in orbit, Mr. Chairman. There appears to be no further action at this time.'

"Let's go home, hon. You need to rest up and conserve your energy for when the shit hits the fan," said Carla. I agreed and we exited the pod.

"I wish I knew what sensory equipment the Crustan's have at their disposal. I'm concerned they'll be able to pick up the safe places where all the people are."

The safe places, accessed through a maze of caves carved out by the planet's evolutionary process over millions of years, went deep into the base of the mountain. Our resident geologist estimated Hera-soter's age to be three billion years, a bit younger than the Earth. The two moons, which orbited at various distances, provided a similar stability to the oceans as the Earth's moon afforded our old home planet.

"We will have to wait and see. There's not much more we can do—what do the people have for protection?" asked Carla.

"The four groups, each with one-hundred and fifty people, are scattered throughout the various caverns of the cave system and ten people in each group have high-powered lasers from the Andromeda's armory. The problem is the lasers will not keep their charge forever and the electrical battery backup systems need to be used sparingly by each group."

"But they do have good food and water supplies?" she asked.

"Each group, on rations could last about two weeks."

"What about the antimatter canon?"

"Lieutenant Sparkle will handle the controls from the bunker. If that fails his own lasers are all we have left."

I lay on my bed and closed my eyes. There would be no sleep for me as we waited for the Crustans to embark on some sort of action. I cursed my stupidity regarding the broken leg. Some lost weight, due to lack of proper eating and lack of sleep showed—my ribs stuck out more than I could ever remember and dark rings had appeared under my eyes.

Carla came in from the kitchen and held out one of the super bars from our pod's supply of emergency rations. I popped it into my mouth and swallowed. The highly concentrated vitamin content would release me from the need for normal food for the next thirty-six hours.

She sat down on the bed beside me and ran her hand through my hair. "You really need to get some sleep."

"You know as well as I do how impossible that will be," I mumbled.

Happydoo came into the room. After the warship's pass over the village he had taken it upon himself to check on the forest dwellers. Lucy and Charley looked on the android as a personal friend. I'm not sure if their concept of human beings could tell the difference between us and the androids. Happydoo's actions mirrored ours so closely it negated any attempt to explain artificial intelligence to them. His personal tuition, in helping them grasp our language rivaled Laura Samuels who admirably performed the task of school mistress, to the two dozen forest dwellers who came to school three days a week.

"How are our furry friends?" I asked.

'They are nervous about the return of the Crustans and want to help when the fireworks start but I told them on no account must they show themselves, Master Beckett.'

"I find it strange that the Crustans never ventured away from the lake while they used their station."

'I think they were only interested in the water. Their prospecting is likely to involve asteroids, Master Beckett—much like ours did before the Relocation Project.'

"How large is the local clan of forest dwellers?" I asked.

'I believe they number about fifty-five, Master Beckett. I asked Charley if there were any others that he knew of. He told me several families left a long time ago because of leadership differences but he has no idea what happened to them. They never forage for more than fifty miles —none of them have a wanderlust or pioneer instinct.'

"The Crustans will use them as target practice if they're discovered," said Carla.

'I did inform them of the dangers, Mrs. Carla. They will move out of the area if things get really bad.'

I heard a scuff of boots outside the entrance to the bedroom and Lieutenant Sparkle knocked on the entrance.

'Mr. Chairman, I think we need to get back to the command pod. The alien fleet is making a move.'

I cursed. "Let's go and see what these bastards are up to."

*

Half an hour later we moved down into the bunker and switched on the holo-platform. The alien ships did not need landing modules but swooped down, toward a section of land void of trees on the lake shore, to land their craft. I made a mental note to ask Commander Cruse if the Prime Endeavor could do this, which would set it apart from our Andromeda. I remembered the nerds in the Relocation Project had been busy with the concept of terrestrial landings for a craft as large as the PE.

The Relocation log needed to be updated and it took a moment to open the holo-file for a quick entry about the enemy's latest movements. I left the file open on standby so further entries could be made in the event of a status change.

69

We watched as four of the seven craft landed in clouds of dust, interspersed with scorched vegetation thrown high into the air, which obscured most of our vision for a time. When the dust settled the Crustans poured out of the craft to form four squads of combatants, all togged out in their cumbersome suits. In total they numbered sixty-four.

The helmets did not close off their faces but provided a mask to cover their nostrils, which I assumed supplied a hydro-rich mixture of air. From our previous experience we discovered the aliens could breathe our atmosphere but the dry air limited their performance. It appeared Lieutenant Sparkles' original assessment of the situation might be correct.

"They must have figured out the Andromeda poses no threat. The antimatter canon remains our most effective defense against the fleet but if they discover where it operates from we could be in some trouble," I said.

'They appear to be preparing to march to the village, Mr. Chairman.'

"I'm not quite sure, what we should do—is there anything tactical the Diamond 1000 military program can offer?" I asked.

'Not specifically, Sir, but my advice is to take out the four ships at the lake with the antimatter cannon.'

"Don't forget they still have three more ships in orbit—I believe the three have settled on an orbit much closer to the surface. What is the distance, Mickey?"

There are two ships in geo-orbit at three thousand kilometers, Mr. Chairman. The third appears to have left the immediate area. I believe they may be checking out the presence of the Prime Endeavor. I have alerted Commander Cruse to the possibility.'

I considered the position. "If we use the anti-matter canon on the four ground ships it may give our weapon's position away but at least the enemy's attack force will have been significantly reduced."

"Which will leave us with the two ships in orbit and the ground force of combatants," said Carla.

"The anti-matter canon may be able to deal with the two orbiting ships before they pinpoint its position."

"How effective would it be on the enemy soldiers," she asked.

Lieutenant Sparkle interrupted. *'The anti-matter is not efficient with small targets unless they are completely composed of metal substances. I doubt whether it will have any effect at all, Mrs. Conroy.'*

I needed to make a swift decision. "So the canon is only useful to us in taking out the enemy ships—we need to do it right away and trust we can neutralize their entire fleet."

"And hope the Prime Endeavor is able to deal with the remaining ship," added Carla.

Mickey made his own observation. *'It would perhaps be expedient to take out the two orbiting ships first, Boss. They must have us in their sights, as it is.'*

"Good idea, Mickey. It'll take the four ground ships time to discover the cannon's position and adjust their weapons to destroy it."

Lieutenant Sparkle sat down at the console beside me. *'I will handle this, Mr. Chairman.'*

The android called on Mickey for the specific coordinates and signed in with the auxiliary computer on the mountaintop.

'I will keep the beam concentrated on the center of the first ship until the antimatter reaction begins—the vacuum of space will do the rest for us.'

A second holo-platform activated above the console and we could see the two ships, at a distance of one-hundred kilometers of each other, in silent and perfect geo-synchronous orbit.

Sparkle sat with his one bionic hand on a signal-input port and the fingers of his other on a keypad. He typed in the coordinates with swift determination and his blue orb-eyes pulsed with intensity.

∞∞

EIGHT

Confrontation

The lieutenant stared intently at the holo-platform. *'Here we go'*.

The holo showed no visible evidence of the cannon's concentrated ray of particles and for a moment there was no change in the enemy's status. Moments later, a sudden conflagration of light lit up the sky and the first craft began to dissolve before our eyes.

The lieutenant moved the beam with immediate effect onto the other ship and with the tap of a key, locked the anti-matter beam onto the craft's propulsion plume as it took immediate, evasive action. It can never be known what the commanders of the enemy vessels thought in their last moments but Mickey picked up a hysterical communication to the ground ships. The second craft took a matter of seconds to break apart, which had given its commander the opportunity for a possible one-word warning to their comrades on the ground. All four grounded warships tried to expedite a hasty startup of their propulsion systems.

The alien combatants scrambled to get away from their craft as the vessels vibrated in the buildup of power for immediate launch but it appeared the drive systems were not sufficiently recharged for optimum takeoff. The combatants spread out away from the lake and scuttled into the forest to gain the protection of the tree canopy.

Sparkle adjusted the position of the beam and targeted the first ship on the ground. He concentrated the anti-matter beam directly onto what appeared to be the ship's bridge area. As with the two orbiting vessels it lit up like a supernova and the upper area began to dissolve.

"What will happen with the nukes aboard," I asked.

They will be completely neutralized by the anti-matter,' said Sparkle.

"That's a relief," said Carla. "Imagine the amount of energy released. We might not have stood a chance, even here in the bunker."

The second vessel shuddered and popped up into the air but its power appeared insufficient for a safe launch and it collided heavily into the third vessel. This gave Sparkle time to target this ship and it too dissolved into a mess of liquefied metal. The fourth ship reached optimum power and shot vertically into the air but the antimatter beam locked onto its rocket plume. Within the space of minutes the enemy fleet had been neutralized. This increased our chances of survival by eighty percent.

Now the battle against the Crustan combatants would begin. Carla and I couldn't believe the swiftness with which the destruction of the warships had taken place.

"Well done Lieutenant. Once again, your ability to operate effectively in a tight situation comes to light—and by the way, I'm still waiting for you to tell me how you escaped the explosion of the first Warship, before our arrival on Herasoter."

'Thank you, Mr. Chairman—but that story will have to wait for a more convenient opportunity for me to tell it. We have a difficult task ahead.'

"A task in which you will need to play a significant role, Lieutenant," said Carla.

'Indeed, Mrs. Conroy. I have spoken to the security personnel and chief Spanner has set up a means for us to keep the laser weapons charged. I too will need to set up a source of power when my charge runs down—my laser capability will consume a large amount of energy if prolonged. This may present some difficulties if I have to leave the pod area and find myself in a tight situation.'

"I know you and Mrs. Conroy have had some discussions regarding the use of the security personnel. How do you propose to handle the attack, Lieutenant?"

'With Mrs. Conroy's permission I have arranged for twenty of our trained security people to set up a perimeter around the pods, Mr. Chairman. They are already digging themselves in. We will wait for the Crustans to approach. The remaining lasers have been left with capable people in the safe places.'

"What about heavy ordinance, firing beneath the force field's overhead protection?"

'We don't have anything to help us there, Mr. Chairman. All our people can do is to stay down in their respective foxholes. The pods can withstand quite an extreme force but it's limited.'

One of the security personnel knocked on the door of the pod. I remembered him—Mike Hunter— from our excursion to the Solar Star, an asteroid ferry which disappeared, when we still mined the Belt. Unbeknown to us at the time, the vessel contained Ozzy and his Orbitron.

Hunter nodded at me and addressed Sparkle. "We are ready Lieutenant. Everyone is armed with a laser and Chief Spanner has rigged up a power-cord to each foxhole so the weapons can be charged."

'Thank you Mr. Hunter. Is each person set up with comms?'

"As per our discussion, Lieutenant. You should be able talk to us from the console."

Sparkle's plans appeared solid. We had initially discussed moving out of the area but the Crustans would certainly track us down. If our last stand at the pods failed we hoped the aliens would think we represented Earth's total compliment.

A sudden impact reverberated throughout the pod as a missile exploded on the overhead protective shield.

'The Crustan attack has started—I would suggest you and Mrs. Conroy move down into the bunker,' said Sparkle.

Happydoo, always the faithful valet, followed us down the ladder. 'I will be your last line of defense, Master Beckett—please set me into aggressive mode and let's hope it doesn't come to that.'

The android turned his back and bent over to allow me access to the flap of synthetic skin on his lower back. I made the appropriate adjustment and we sat down at the auxiliary console, with its two holo-platforms. I could monitor the outside progress from camera's set up inside the pod and outside on its roof.

"Here they come," said Carla. The hologram on the platform gave us a 3-D, 360 degrees view of our surroundings. A group of enemy soldiers crept along the approach path to the quadrangle. They looked furtively around in an effort to spot any form of resistance, their large red eyes visible behind the atmospheric masks. The leader held a device, which I took to be a heat sensor, in his hand and swung it around in a semi-circle. When the device pointed toward our pod he stopped to scrutinize the readings and gave a command to the soldiers behind him. They all dropped to the ground with their short, stubby weapons at the ready.

"I can vouch for their hand-weapons," I said.

Sparkle spoke softly through the comm. *'They've spotted us, Mr. Chairman.'*

"I'll leave you to command your men as you see fit, Lieutenant,"

'Thank you for the heads up, Sir. I've linked into a scenario in my program. I think they have realized the pod area has a protective shield over it. They can possibly see our forms on infra-red. More enemy soldiers are appearing from the opposite direction—we are surrounded and I count fifty-five combatants, including two leaders.'

"With the knowledge of the destruction of their fleet they will be ready to fight to the death, Sparkle—there will be no quarter given."

'I am aware of that, sir. We are ready for the fight.'

We continued to watch as the enemy force crawled further toward the foxholes and then stopped. Lieutenant Sparkle, in a calm voice, issued a command. 'Come to firing position and pick a target. The enemy is on the ground in an attempt to minimize their profiles—when I give the order, fire at will.'

Our guards in the foxholes positioned themselves and made ready to fire on the enemy. The mounds of red sand, dug up from the foxholes gave our people some minimal protection, but I felt a growing concern for our lack of numbers.

Sparkle did not wait any longer. *'Fire at will.'*

All hell broke loose. The Crustans soon realized the protective field did not extend to the ground and concentrated their fire on the mounds of sand. Each alien soldier produced its own personal protective energy field—a capability we had not anticipate. Our hand-lasers bounced uselessly off, to scorch up the earth around them.

Lieutenant Sparkle's voice remained calm. *'Make sure your weapon is on maximum power and keep firing at one particular spot of their body armor.'*

I heard cries of pain come from some of the foxholes. The enemy fire literally burned some of the people through the sand. I tried to pick up the exact location of these holes and found three stations where laser weapons no longer pointed over the mounds.

"We are losing people, Sparkle," I shouted.

'Their hand weaponry is much stronger than ours, Mr. Chairman. Our people need to concentrate their fire in one place. The resultant

buildup of heat will eventually burn a hole through the energy-fields.'

My blood ran cold as two more Crustans arrived from between the village homes. Between them they carried a larger weapon. I knew this would be bad for us.

"Sparkle? Do you see the heavy artillery?"

'I see it, Sir. It's time for me to go into action. We have lost twelve people and our hand-lasers are not making a dent.'

"What can we do to help?" I asked.

'Use your CCT to keep me updated on the area outside of my vision, Mr. Chairman—position and numbers of enemy soldiers. I will have to leave the pod. While using lasers my charge will only last for ten minutes at the most.'

"Good luck, Lieutenant. Give 'em hell."

∞∞

NINE

Victory is Sweet

I grabbed my CCT, set the pad to my temple and introduced Sparkle's registration number. I heard an immediate click in my mind and knew I had a connection to the android. We watched as the lieutenant slipped out of the door and ran in a half-crouch toward the group of enemy combatants in the quadrangle. I considered he might hide in the doorway of the pod but it appeared the AI had its own ideas about combat.

At a certain point in his headlong flight Sparkle stopped and dropped to the ground. He turned to face several enemy soldiers, who lay on their abdomens, huddled in a group. The stream of laser light shot out from his eyes to rake their position and each personal protective shield collapsed under the beam's intensity. The soldiers screamed in pain and rolled around in an attempt to escape the heat, but in vain.

We took fire from the enemy's heavy artillery and an explosion shook the entire pod, as a missile struck the wall of the command pod above us. All our cameras, however, continued to work and I focused on the situation behind the pod to see several enemy soldiers creep closer to the perimeter. Our guards kept up a concentrated fire but the effort seemed to make little difference as the strength of the enemy's shields protected them. I did not know how much longer we could hold out.

By this time Sparkle, encouraged by his success with a frontal attack aimed his laser at the heavy artillery and they in turn redirected their aim, to target him. The short grass around the androids ankles burst into flame as the canon scored a partial hit. I groaned inwardly as the android went down under a hail of fire from the weapon. Smoke plumed upward from the AI's position and I feared for its survival. A second later, however, Sparkle came up onto his bionic knees and targeted the canon.

The beams shot out again and this time the enemy soldiers burst into flames and the weapon melted, its remains falling uselessly to the ground. The remaining Crustans in the frontal attack, aware of the weapon's destruction, drew back. A few soldiers tried to concentrate some fire on the android but missed as it crawled toward them with lasers raking the quadrangle.

I checked on the rear attack. The enemy, now closer to the perimeter, continued a barrage of laser fire at the foxholes. Our people fought with extreme bravery but could not breach the enemy's protective energy shields and when our weapons failed to turn the tide, the guards threw themselves with fury at the Crustans. I wanted to weep for these brave man and women, who gave their lives to protect us.

"Sparkle, can you still hear me?"

'I can hear you, sir. I have got the front area under control and they are in retreat.'

"I'm glad to hear it but I think we are about to be overrun from the back. The enemy is at the perimeter and our guards are on the brink of defeat."

'I will finish off the rest here and get to the back in a few minutes, Mr. Chairman but I need a charge.'

Happydoo tapped me on the shoulder. 'I will go Master Beckett. I will take one of the energy cables directly to him.'

"You are placing yourself at a huge risk, Happydoo," said Carla.

'It cannot be helped Mrs. Carla—we have run out of options and the lieutenant is our only hope of survival now.'

"Go, quickly and keep as low as you can."

'I'm happy to do that, Master Beckett.'

The android climbed the ladder and opened the trapdoor into the pod. An internal camera picked up the image as it moved to the back of the console to grab a long role of heavy duty energy cable. He moved out of the door on all fours and crawled toward Sparkle who continued to concentrate his beams on the enemy. A Crustan laser lit up the area where he lay and the grass burst into flames, which resulted in a haze smoke. For a moment I lost sight of them.

"I think Sparkle has taken a direct hit," said Carla.

I peered at the hologram in front of us. "If he's been incapacitated we are done for."

The smoke cleared and I saw Happydoo, with one end of the cable inserted into a console port and the other end clutched in his hand, still on the crawl towards Sparkle's position. Another laser lit up the area where Sparkle had been but I could no longer see him—only a patch of blackened grass.

"Where's Sparkle, hon—can you see him at all?"

I watched Happydoo change direction, still with energy cord in hand. "I think he has changed his position."

We tried to see through the haze but it obscured the area and I could not make out his status. Happydoo crawled into the thick of the swirling smoke and disappeared from view. I switched to the cameras on the other side of the pod. Several Crustans stood with their weapons pointed at the foxholes and I knew our defenses were breached. All our guards, who fought so gallantly with their inferior weapons, now lay dead or wounded. Our situation looked grim.

With the Relocation Log still open my voice sounded a little shaky as I made a comment:

A quick update on our status—the enemy has surrounded the command pod. It is beginning to look as though they may overwhelm us.....

I switched back to the frontal attack, and with most of the haze lifted, I noticed the enemy no longer fired on the lieutenant's last known position.

Ozzy's emergency distress signaling device hung round my neck and I fingered it for a brief moment. The likelihood of our alien friend, performing a rescue, rated zero. I rubbed my eyes and peered at the holo-platform, to see if the enemy still commanded any area in front of the command pod and saw mounds of burning alien flesh, entangled in smoldering body armor. Sparkle and Happydoo, however, appeared to have disappeared from view, so I switched to the back area again.

Happydoo stood behind the lieutenant, holding his android companion in a tight embrace. My puzzled conclusion soon found the reason— Sparkle's legs, below the knee-joints, no longer existed. He could not walk so Happydoo had carried him from the front, around the side of the command pod, to face the enemy at the back. I could see the energy cable attached to the lieutenant's back. As we continued to watch in awe, the two laser beams shot out and decimated the Crustans, who stood gaping at the two androids.

I grabbed a crutch, climbed up the ladder and hobbled to the door to squint out at the smoky scene.

Carla appeared behind me. "Have we won?"

I looked out at the quad to see the scorched grass and burned mounds of Crustan flesh. It took a few moments to get around the side to see a heart-warming scenario at the back—not the mounds of dead Crustan combatants, but the two androids seated on the ground, gazing at each other in awe. Happydoo sat with the lieutenant supported between his knees and Sparkle's back leaned against my valet's chest. I am almost certain I saw a glimmer of relief and respect reflected in each of their eyes.

'That was a piece of cake, wasn't it Lieutenant?' said Happydoo.

'*A walk in the park,*' answered Sparkle.

I ruffled my valet's hard, stubbly hair. "You both saved us from a horrible defeat."

'*Unfortunately, Mr. Chairman, It came at a considerable cost and I'm not referring to the loss of my legs.*'

The moment sobered me. I moved toward the foxholes and the smell of scorched flesh filled my nostrils. "They all fought a brilliant fight," I said.

Carla came and stood at my side. "They died that we might live. We will honor their sacrifice with a memorial— it must never be forgotten."

*

Three days later, with the area cleaned up and the remainder of our village people settled back in their homes, we held a memorial service for the dead. Only three of our guards survived the ordeal and would take some time to recover from the burns they received in the skirmish. The Crustan remains also received a burial in a separate place and I wanted to put up a stone to mark the area but most of the people felt it a lost gesture.

"I thought it a good idea to remind us never to be complacent about the enemy," I said.

"I'm sure we'll never forget the possibility of them paying us another visit. Hon. I don't think the people need to be reminded by the physical presence of a Crustan cemetery."

"I wonder what happened to the third which left the fleet before destruction of their ships. They must have heard their comrades were in trouble."

She raised her eyebrows. "Well, they've not returned. I can only think they were frightened out of their crustacean skulls at the destruction of all their comrades."

"I guess we'll find out soon enough. I sent Happydoo to find out if Mickey has detected any sign of a foreign craft. Here he comes and appears to be in a hurry."

I could see the android in a hastened gait, approaching our home. He disappeared from view and then a burst through the front entrance.

'Master Beckett—Mrs. Carla—good news. Mickey has received a message from the Prime Endeavor.'

∞∞

TEN

The Prime Endeavor

One week later the prime Endeavor entered orbit. At first, the starship appeared as a streak of light but when its velocity slowed down, the ship's hull glowed in the rays of Pegasi 51. Everyone gathered in the quadrangle to watch it circle the planet until it matched Hera-soter's rotation.

I sat at the console. "Beckett Conroy to Commander Cruse. We see you clearly Prime Endeavor, when will you be ready to enter the atmosphere?"

"Commander Cruse to Dr. Conroy: we will make entry in ten minutes. Where would you have us put the ship down?"

I anticipated the question and together with the Relocation committee, in consideration of the prime Endeavor's massive size, we decide to use the open field beside the lake. The cleanup of the metal-slop remains of the Crustan warships took us a few days, but the sizable opening would accommodate the starship. I gave the location to Commander Cruse and told everyone to walk toward the lake. The possible return of the Crustans still haunted us but Mickey posited it would be a long time before the enemy would make an appearance again.

The excitement amongst the village people had remained palpable for the entire week. The forest dwellers turned out in force to join us in the welcome of mother Earth's latest gift—the second group of relocation participants to make the epic journey. In my communications with Commander Cruse I established some facts regarding the people on board the prime Endeavor.

Cruse confirmed the presence of two important people in the group—Freda Banning, once my Uncle Sid's personal secretary, and James Hyde—my father. Dr. Padraig Conroy—my dad, the senior geneticist at the World Genetic Foundation, had changed his name in the aftermath of his secret experiment on consciousness transfer. Part of my agreement to lead the Relocation Project hinged on the inclusion of my dad and Freda, now his wife, when they felt ready to make the move.

Needless to say my enthusiasm to be reunited with them knew no bounds. The third person, whom I expected might be on the journey, related to a major incident which took place on the Andromeda during our relocation—the tragic mutiny and consequent death of my XO, Gary Pearson—his brother, Colin. Colin Pearson, Gary's brother had been involved in the plan to displace Carla and I from leadership. While the Andromeda had been under reconstruction, Pearson's job involved the installation of certain protocols, to be accessed by a sign-in procedure. But for Happydoo's discovery of the wicked plan, both Carla and I would be dead. My XO's connections to people in The Administration sealed a place on the next journey for his brother.

With the possibility of his inclusion, and before its confirmation by Commander Cruse, the Relocation Committee decided we would set up a judicial system, to deal with possible future crimes committed by the village people—Colin Pearson would be incarcerated on his arrival and his trial would begin. The two lawyers in our original group and an attorney with Cruse's group would be sworn in as the presiding judges, to bring our new legal system into being. Preparations for a banquet, to honor the Prime Endeavor's compliment and to bring them up to speed on their new home planet, had kept Carla busy for several days before the arrival. The new people would need to continue the use of their starship as living quarters, until we built homes to accommodate them.

Our walk to the lake took twenty minutes. Carla turned to me and smiled. "I guess you will welcome Commander Cruse onto the Establishment Committee?"

"I will certainly give her the opportunity but only when she is ready."

"It took us months to acclimatize and adjust to the different conditions. It will be the same for them," she said.

Another thought entered my mind. "According to Cruse they never saw any alien craft. I wonder what happened to the one craft that left before the alien fleet attacked us."

"You're worried there will be a return of the enemy, don't you, hon?"

"I do, sweetheart. I can't help thinking we have won a battle but the war is yet to come."

"She squeezed my hand. "Let's not worry about it now—the next hour will be epic in our lives. Mickey has his eye in the sky so we should relax and enjoy this home-coming of the travelers."

I knew she was right but the negative thoughts still niggled.

I stopped the people at the edge of the lake, about one kilometer from the chosen landing site and we all sat down to wait. Lucy and Charley approached us with their usual respect and sat on their haunches close to us with their eyes to the ground.

"Come and sit beside us," said Carla. They crawled toward us with huge grins on their faces. Charley waited for me to place my hand on his head before he parked his fury body up against my leg.

"Charley, him happy for Charman Buckitt."

I reached out and ruffled the long hair on his head. "You will meet my father today, Charley." I said.

The forest dweller bared his teeth in the imitation of a human smile, much like chimps used to do on Earth before their complete disappearance from the forests. Few remained in captivity at the time of our departure. The plan to clone certain extinct animal species remained the hope for the future and the Relocation Project catered for a number of other important genus groups.

"Charley, him father too."

"I know, my friend. You are the fine father of four strapping young boys and six girls."

Yes, Charman Buckitt. Charley him strong father."

Carla grinned at me and we laughed. The forest dwellers lived a simple life in the trees of the forest and apart from teaching them the language we left any further advancement up to them. A new partnership between our group and theirs, saw to the abundance of game and fruit we all enjoyed. Maybe in time they would progress to our more modern standards but for now they remained intelligent pets with whom we developed a good relationship. They had become a part of our family.

All eyes stared into the sky as the bright red flare of the prime Endeavor's descent grew closer and with a sudden bang the noise of the massive engines hit us. Everyone raised their hands to cover ears—Lucy emitted a wail and sank to the ground to hold her head with shaking hands. Carla rubbed the fur on the back of her neck in a gesture of comfort. Charley fixed his eyes on the vessel and his mouth hung wide open. Never before had they seen anything as large as the PE and it overwhelmed them.

The roar of the engines grew louder as the huge craft hovered above the ground, lining up its perimeter for a sudden drop to the grass below. Tufts of small bush swirled upward and debris shot out in a wide radius. Some of the village people closed their eyes for protection and waited for the craft to touch down. I saw a host of massive claw-like appendages appear from the underside to extend down and outward, to support the weight of the craft—unlike the Andromeda which could only dock beside a platform.

Our long wait had come to an end. The Prime Endeavor represented the most modern of spacecraft ever built and its rugged, gutsy lines displayed every inch of its magnificent capabilities. It epitomized the brilliance in technology and engineering skills of its builders. The vessel took up the entire area of field once occupied by the four of the alien warships. The craft settled on the myriad of stilts beneath it and with one accord the roar of the engines ceased.

The dust and debris floated down to be caught up in the slight on-shore breeze from the lake. We all surged forward toward the ship and after several minutes formed a semicircle in front of the main hatch to wait. Moments later the hatch opened and two figures stood there in awe, their eyes taking in the crowd and surrounding area. A ramp extended from beneath the hatch toward the ground and everyone cheered. The two figures seemed frozen in time, unable to move.

∞∞

ELEVEN

Reunited with Family

It is hard to explain the emotion I felt. My dreams always depicted past Earth scenes in which my loved ones often played a part and I could not remember once having dreamed about our new location. With my heart pounding I grabbed Carla's hand and we surged up the ramp toward them, in recognition of the two faces—Freda and my dad.

My father stuttered out a word of greeting.

"Beckett, Carla—God, I've waited so long for this."

The moment overwhelmed me as I embrace him. "Dad—is this real?"

Freda embraced the two of us, lost for words. Carla stood back and smiled. A horde of faces appeared around us from within the ship. Everyone cheered so loud I'm sure many almost lost their voices. This was the most memorable moment I can remember. After a few moments I became conscious of an attractive lady, with white hair and startling, steel-blue eyes, standing behind my dad. She possessed a slender figure for her age and wore a smart blue tight-fit suit with a president commander's pendant, above the left breast.

"Dr. Beckett Conroy?" I recognized the distinct voice from our recent contacts with the Prime Endeavor.

"President Commander Cruse—what a pleasure it is to finally meet you," I said.

Her smile revealed sparkling white teeth. "This is my husband, Philip Cruse, Chief Executive Supervisor of Prime Endeavor City." She stepped aside and a tall man with short gray hair stepped up to shake my hand. I in turn introduced Carla and each member of the Establishment Committee. A cough behind me caused me to turn my head. Charley and Lucy stood there patiently awaiting an introduction.

"And who are these creatures?" asked Cruse. I could see she felt unsure about their presence. I introduced the forest dwellers who knelt in complete humility with their eyes lowered to the ground. I asked Commander Cruse to place her hand on Charley's head which, after some hesitation, she did. The forest dweller jumped up and to her surprise, embraced her. Lucy remained kneeling in the background. Carla stepped up to explain our history with the creatures and praised their intelligence in the mastering of our language. The PE's people were enraptured.

"Are you ready to come into the village? We have so much to talk about," I said.

Commander Cruse looked back to her people in the entrance. "Who's ready to step onto firm soil?"

The corridor, about ten feet wide, brimmed with City people and crew. They all shouted their approval with one accord.

"I have arranged for our security to remain for the time being. But I think everyone is dying to experience the planet—it is absolutely beautiful—what have you called it again?" asked Cruse.

"Hera-soter—Hera, I'm sure you will know this—is the wife of the mythological god, Zeus and 'soter' is a Greek word for savior."

"Wonderfully apt, Dr. Conroy. I love it," she said.

"Please call me Beckett and I'm sure my wife will insist you call her Carla."

"Call me Rebecca—I'm also sure my husband would ask you to call him Philip."

We surged down the ramp to the ground and proceeded to walk toward the village. My dad and Freda followed on behind holding the hands of Charley and Lucy, who after a short introduction, seemed to have taken each other into their hearts at first sight. I could hear Charley giving his version of how Carla and I met their clan through the confrontation with the dinabird. Their teacher, Laura Samuels walked beside them to help with appropriate expressions, when Charley drew a blank.

"I need to ask a question of you, Rebecca—are you able to print android accessories?"

"We certainly can. What do you need?"

I breathed a sigh of relief. "Our printer never made it through the initial trip. The people's representative, an android by name of Sparkle, lost his legs in the recent skirmish with those alien invaders I told you about."

"You must tell us all about the incident," said Philip.

I will but our Lieutenant Sparkle needs a new set of legs. He's been hobbling along on his knees with the help of two canes for a while and I'm sure he'll be ecstatic to hear you can help him."

Rebecca's eyes opened wide. "This android is military?"

I related how Sparkle came to be on the project and how we at first did not understand the appointment by Dr. Abrams, the Relocation Project director.

"When we get a chance to sit down and have a discussion I'll tell you what a blessing he has been to us," I said.

A total of two thousand, four hundred people poured off the Prime Endeavor and a long column formed behind us. All the new comers were beside themselves with regard to the planet's beauty and could not get over how closely Hera-soter resembled Earth. One hundred crew and security stayed on board.

On our arrival at the village the newcomers were greatly impressed by the neat homes. The scorched and buckled walls of the pods caught Philip's eye and he wanted to know if the flight through the atmosphere had done the damage. The quadrangle did not appear to be big enough to accommodate everybody and I asked Rebecca to explain to her people they could move freely amongst all the homes and buildings but no one was to leave the perimeter of the village without a guide.

After a quick inspection of the pods we walked over to our home. Due to the small area available I encouraged only my dad and Freda, together with Rebecca and her husband, to stay and talk.

"We will arrange a sit-down with our combined executive to seek out how we will all approach the future," I said.

Carla enjoyed the aspect of entertainment the visit provided. "Happydoo, can you rustle up some fruit-juice and palma-nuts for us please?"

'I will be happy to do it for you, Mrs. Carla.'

We seated ourselves on the rustic furniture provided by the carpenters in our group. Rebecca's excitement, after so many years in space became evident when she placed her hands over her eyes and sat for several moments, to allow the emotion of the moment to settle. Carla sat beside her and placed an arm around her shoulders.

Rebecca removed her hands to reveal tears. "Please give me a moment."

Philip smiled. "It's been hard for all of us—such a long time—not knowing if we would ever make it here."

"Carla and I fully understand." I said.

A few moments later Rebecca recovered her composure and apologized. "Now tell us about your flight and these aliens you spoke of earlier."

I needed to ask one more question before the sage of our trip could be told. "Do you have a Colin Pearson aboard—working in IT, perhaps?"

Rebecca gave me a surprised look. "Yes—that is, we did. It's a strange story."

"What happened to him?"

She looked to her husband for encouragement. "Go on," he said.

"He committed suicide a short time after we received our first confirmation of your successful arrival on the planet. I shared the good news with everyone and the next thing he came to my office and asked a strange question."

My intrigue grew. "What did he ask?"

"He wanted to know who was in charge on Hera-soter. When I told him it was Chairman Beckett Conroy he turned absolutely pale. The next morning we found him dead in his cubicle."

I told her all about Gary Pearson, the Andromeda's XO and the plan to have Carla and I eliminated and stressed that had it not been for Happydoo, we would not have survived. I explained how Gary's brother, Colin, changed the hibernation protocols during the reconstruction of the Andromeda. They sat transfixed and listened to the full story of our journey. When I came to the bizarre meeting with Ozzy and how fortuitous it had been for our survival, their mouths were agape. To end the sage I mentioned our survival of the initial alien onslaught and arrival on the planet. Their eyes opened wider when we related the Crustan return and recent battle.

"Good God," said Philip. "Remind me never to tangle with your androids."

I laughed. "You are probably wondering about my leg." I explained the ordeal of the mountain and the establishment of the anti-matter canon.

"Can you arrange to get the lieutenant over to the ship?" asked Rebecca. "I will have our chief engineer measure his legs and print them. You should come too—we have a rapid bone and tissue healer on board."

"I would love to do a tour of the Prime Endeavor—I will certainly take you up on the offer," I said.

My dad and Freda shared their story and we talked about old times.

Happydoo popped his head into the room. 'Greetings, Master Padraig.'

My dad stood, walked to the door and embraced the android. "I am so happy to see, my old friend."

Happydoo's service as a valet to our family spanned one hundred and fifty years.

Rebecca and Philip gave us a curious glance. I took it my father's assumed name still identified him as a professor who taught at the Quantum State University, back on Earth. They had no idea of his real identity.

"It's time for me to resume my real name again—I've never bonded with the name of James Hyde, anyway. Freda and I thought it better to wait until we arrived here before telling anyone."

He went on to explain the reason for the name change—how the breakthrough, during his time of involvement at the World Genetic Foundation, placed his life in imminent danger. He returned to active life in the science community several years later as Dr. James Hyde and pioneered the concept of consciousness transfer.

Rebecca's jaw dropped open. "I never knew the real history behind your breakthrough."

My dad nodded. "I gave the telomere integrity extension research over to my son for further development and, as I always expected, he did wonders with the discovery."

"So I'll have to call you Padraig, now?" asked Rebecca.

"I would prefer it," he answered.

Happydoo broke the moment's tension. 'I will be Happy to refer to you as Dr. Padraig Conroy, Master Padraig—it seems to come naturally to me'.

We all laughed. Philip said he would make an announcement to the people of the Prime Endeavor, with regard to the change of my dad's name, to avoid any confusion.

The shadow of night crept over our side of the planet and all the ship's people decided to retire back to their vessel. Charley and Lucy wanted to go back with my dad and Freda but Laura Samuels managed to get it into the forest dwellers heads that nobody was going to leave the planet— they would all be back in the morning.

Carla and I retired to bed with our senses on overload. I hoped I would not wake up in the morning and find it all to be a dream.

∞∞

TWELVE

The Cave

On Hera-soter, the days turned into weeks and the small community grew into a resourceful group of pioneer settlers with one aim—to reclaim the flow of daily life as experienced on Earth before our relocation. This was not as easy as one would think despite the knowledge of our modern technology and ideas. It takes time to re-establish routines which lead to the building of a civilization. I had forgotten to ask Rebecca Cruse an important question—did they encounter the surviving enemy warship, on route into the Pegasi 51 solar system?

On their second day with us Carla reminded me.

"We encountered no such ship anywhere in the proximity of the constellation," she answered.

"That's odd—they left here a short while before the destruction of the fleet and we all assumed they were sent to go and check out the Prime Endeavor."

"They may have left for their space-dimension—where ever that is," said Carla.

"We'll have to wait and see. One thing we can bet on, though—they'll be back again. It's possible they returned, saw the destruction of their friends and got the hell out of our space."

Rebecca looked thoughtful. "Your Master Control Computer would not have been able to pick up a distant heat signature due to all the scattered debris, so it's quite possible they returned for a brief period to witness what happened."

"We need to plan for another confrontation—the Crustans will not give up easily. I need to consult with Ozzy, to see what we can do."

Ozzy's diminishing visits to our planet revealed the alien's limited time allocated to the universe under his observation. With thousands of species, all at different stages of evolution, his increase in obligations must have been phenomenal. His last visit, subsequent to the failed Crustan invasion of Hera-soter, and days before the arrival of the Prime Endeavor, provided us with a few ideas. The antimatter canon remained our main hope of survival but should the enemy send and overwhelming force, even several such weapons might not help us. We could only hope the war between Lumbria and Crusta held them at bay.

Philip's engineers worked tirelessly with Herbert Matheson and Chief Spanner to construct a second canon. With the resources of the PE, came the establishment of more efficient facilities for our village. A clinic for the sick and injured became indispensable to the small community as the heavier gravity and unknown toxicities, indigenous in the new environment, took its toll on the more adventurist members. Our total compliment now exceeded three-thousand, two hundred people.

On a cloudy day in the sixth year of our establishment program Carla and I, with a partiality for further exploration of the new planet, decided to take a hiatus from the leadership role. Rebecca and Philip stepped in to take up the reigns for a period of time while we took a trip across the waters to a nearby Island. One of the perks, which came with the PE afforded us the opportunity to travel the distance in style by use of its survey module, a nifty antigrav craft. It could take four people comfortably and reach heights of about five thousand feet at a speed of Mach two.

Happydoo accompanied us. His built-in survey equipment could map the terrain. The android would also be a great help with setting up a camp and our comfort requirements. Despite the PE's auto-dress fabricator facility we decided to wear the clothes designed and made from animal skins, now a budding industry in our growing village economy. Over time most members of our community wore natural clothes, as we called them. The auto-dress equipment would only be used for special requirements. I took a hand-laser with as a precaution but determined to use a bow and arrow arrangement, produced by the local forest dwellers, for hunting—we would eat off the land.

Carla's excitement could not be contained. On the day of our departure for the island we called Tall Mountain she huddled beside me as the antigrav made ready to takeoff.

"I can't wait to see what's on the island. It's been a long time since you and I had a bit of down-time together, hon."

"The place has always intrigued me," I said. "There are only a few of them and in time we should have them all mapped and surveyed."

'How long do you intend for us to stay, Master Beckett?'

"About five days—it should not take you long to compile your record while we explore some of those caves up on the mountain."

The antigrav took only a few minutes to make the flight across. We picked a site beside a small, inland lake where several different types of animal scattered as the antigrav settled down in the short, reddish grass. Most of the fauna appeared to be herbivores, much the same as the continent on which our community had established itself. Evidence of the dreaded dinabird could also be seen in a few of the trees and tall bush, scattered over the flat area, below the mountain. Dinabirds, predatory in nature, fed on the flesh of most animals.

A large boar-like creature, a flesh-eater with a row of short tusks on each side of its snout about the size of a hippo, roamed the forests in constant search for herbivores like the Barakis. The Barakis, the animal more like a buffalo but quite harmless, featured as a source of meat for our colony and the forest dwellers. Beyond these there appeared to be no other large animals of note. A host of small critters permeated the forests in abundance as did a variety of colorful bird-like, winged creatures.

On arrival at the lake Happydoo busied himself in the setup of a yurt for Carla and I to sleep in. The android plugged into the antigrav's nuclear power-pack for a charge of his system whenever needed and it provided any power we required. The Chief Engineers on the PE had brought undeveloped schematics for a uranium power-pack and together with Herbert Matheson and Chief Spanner they worked on a new source of energy, to give our three androids long-life power systems. I proposed Happydoo to be the first to receive one of the prototypes but it would still be some time.

"What's our first activity for the day, hon," asked Carla.

"I think we should walk along the shore and explore a possible path up the mountain to those caves. I'm also interested to see if there are any signs of forest dwellers on the island."

'I will finish setting up the yurt before joining you and Mrs. Carla, Master Beckett. I need to find a path to the very top of the mountain so a 360 degree survey can be done.'

We left the android to complete his task and wandered, hand in hand, along the shoreline. I loved the beautiful dark blue color of the uncontaminated water in the lake and the many different shades of vibrant colors vested in the flora. We came across a river which filtered down from the mountain and into the body of water, which appeared clean, fresh and drinkable. The river formed an estuary which supported a host of plant life and small fish. But for the different hues of color, we could have been back on Earth in the days when the magnetic field still gave its life-saving protection.

51 Pegasus sat high in the sky and the heat of the day began to tell on us.

"Let's take a quick swim," said Carla. She stripped off her clothes and walked into the shallows. I followed her lead and we enjoyed the cool refreshing feel of the water around our bodies. The appearance of Happydoo brought us back to reality. With some reluctance we returned to the shore to dry ourselves and continue the search for a pathway up the mountainside.

The android took the lead and we made our way through a group of heavy bushes with thorny spikes, which ripped at our clothes. Happydoo broke off branches and giant leaf-stems, to make a path for us while Carla and I toiled up the incline, which got steeper with every step. Eventually we broke through the bushes onto a steep grassy incline and persevered upward, between huge boulders and rocks in search of a stream, which we could hear but not see.

After another few minutes of toil we came across a small brook with tumbling, gurgling water—both Carla and I happily sank to our knees and drank the fresh liquid.

'I can see an easier way for us to get to the cave mouth, Master Beckett.'

"Lead on Valet. We're almost done with all this climbing," I said.

Another ten minutes of scrambling up through a grassy section, between two outcrops brought us to a flat surface, which preceded the entrance to a cave. The opening spanned about ten yards in width and four in height. The most prominent fact alluded to the presence of an animal, which appeared to have been at rest, against one of the inner walls.

"What do you think it is, hon—forest dwellers?"

My eye caught a tuft of fur snagged on the broken end of a leafy branch which might have been used for a bed or as a source of food.

"I'm not quite sure, sweetheart. What do you think, Happydoo?"

'It doesn't look like anything the forest dwellers do, Master Beckett. They sleep in tree-tops—their diet is essentially fruit and meat.'

"That's true," I concluded.

"Whatever it is it has left a trail back here," said Carla. She pointed to strange looking prints in the soft soil of the cave's floor.

"Looks like the footprints of a forest dweller. Turn on your spotlights, Happydoo—let's see if it's in the cave." I readied the laser for quick use in case the unknown animal took umbrage at our presence and attacked. The android's spotlights, situated within the eye-cameras, turned on to cast a brilliant blue light onto the cave walls and floor. The cave appeared to extend back into the mountain for quite a way. I could feel a distinct draft on my face as we progressed deeper.

"I can smell something—it's like decaying vegetation," I said.

Carla sniffed at the air and concurred. "It certainly doesn't smell very good."

We followed the footprints, which became more numerous as the floor descended further into the cave's depths. The going became more slippery due to the water condensation, which dripped from the roof. Carla lost her footing a few times and though we laughed I felt nervous.

The floor levelled out at a depth of about thirty meters to make the going easier and without notice the cave widened into a large cavern.

"I think that smell is rotting flesh," said Car-la.

We moved further into the dark interior. A source of natural daylight, high up in the roof, caught our attention. I now knew where the draft came from.

"That's a natural vent—we have a chimney above us."

Happydoo swept his twin beams around the cavern and stopped on an object built from rock, plumb in the center of the grotto. It looked like an altar of some sort and as the android moved closer to concentrate the light on it, my blood ran cold.

∞∞

THIRTEEN

A Grisly Sight

Carla stifled a scream. The sight before us produced astonishment and fear.

"What is it?" she cried.

"It looks like the sacrifice of a forest dweller," I said.

Carla regained her composure. "So there are forest dwellers in the area."

"It would appear so. Remember how long it took for us to see our first specimen? They are perfectionists when it comes to concealing their presence."

A young forest dweller, its limbs spread-eagled and tied down with vines to tree branches embedded into the sides of the altar, lay face up. A grimace of terror adorned the childlike features and its chest cavity lay exposed.

I peered down at the hapless creature. "All the insides are missing."

'My pedia on ancient tribal cults shows a similar ritual taking place amongst the Inca peoples of ancient South America, Master Beckett.'

"How revolting and barbaric," said Carla.

"This is definitely not practiced by our group. Charley did say some dwellers left a long time ago—according to his grandparents. They may have been more aggressive in their thinking and have started a different culture here."

A sound at the cavern entrance caused us to tear our attention from the altar. At the end of the android's twin beams we saw a group of forest dwellers staring in our direction. As the beams fell on them they took fright and scrambled back along the cave toward the entrance. There may have been thirty or forty of them, I could not be sure, but within seconds they all disappeared.

"We need to get out of here, quickly," said Carla.

"Don't worry, sweetheart—I have the laser."

"We don't want to kill anyone, though. We are the intruders—maybe we can converse with them, like with Charley and Lucy."

"I'll only fire if I have to, hon—but based on the evidence of the sacrifice I doubt whether our reception will be a good one. Let's move out."

We left the cavern with its macabre scene and after a difficult struggle to maintain traction on the ascending floor of the cave we arrived at the entrance, unscathed. The fresh mountain air smelled good as we stepped out into the late afternoon sunshine. We looked around carefully but saw no sign of the forest dwellers so we climbed to the top of the mountain where Happydoo did his 360 degrees survey of the island. The scenery enthralled us.

"Did you record the entire event in the cave, Happydoo?"

'I did, Master Beckett. I assume you will want to rerun the video on the antigrav's holo-platform.'

"As soon as we get back to camp," I said.

An annoying site greeted us on our return to the campsite. The door of the yurt lay a few feet away and it became clear we had become victims of a break-in. Inside, our portable table lay overturned and its contents strewn around, on the floor.

Carla placed her hands on her hips and stared at the mess. "This isn't very nice of them."

"It's predictable. Don't forget they've not seen humans before. Perhaps they're just curious." I said.

"Let's hope they keep their distance. This is all quite unnerving."

'I can repair the door to the yurt, Mrs. Carla. Tonight I will sit in the antigrav and charge my system. If anything transpires I will wake you and Master Beckett.'

Our dinner comprised of local fruit and dried meat—compliments of our rations, before we settled down on a blowup mattress for the night. Happydoo climbed into the antigrav to set up a charge for his system. My one hand rested on the butt of the laser, which I slid under my pillow and after a short chat we both fell into a fitful sleep.

*

In the morning the sun streamed into the yurt and heated the small area to an uncomfortable level. The air-conditioner had not automatically kicked in so I got dressed and went outside to look at the apparatus. Carla followed.

"It appears to be faulty. I'll get Happydoo to look at it," I said.

"I'm going for a pee," she answered.

The hatch of the antigrav slid open and Happydoo appeared.

'Good morning, Master Beckett.'

I greeted him with my usual morning grunt.

"Please have a look at the air-conditioner—it's not working."

The android stepped around the back of the yurt to conduct a quick inspection when we heard Carla cry out. Her voice contained a trace of fear.

"Beckett—quick, help me."

I turned and ran in the direction of her voice. Unfortunately, my laser still lay in the yurt. I considered retrieving it but she sounded anxious—I plunged headlong into the forest and shouted for Happydoo, to bring the laser. The tall forest trees at the back of the camp provided ample cover for any dangerous animals to hide and I chided myself for allowing Carla to go off alone, despite her need for some personal privacy.

She screamed and a panic flooded my usual calm disposition. A flurry of branches and leaves preceded a sudden silence. I stopped to listen, my heart pounding like a sledge hammer. Happydoo caught up and he too stopped to listen. We heard a further, muffled scream accompanied by the shaking of branches.

'I believe the forest dwellers have got Mrs. Carla, Master Beckett.'

I wanted to faint. This could not be happening to us. Horrific thoughts of forest dwellers, with their penchant for sacrifice, crossed my mind before I kicked into survival mode. I needed to trace the footsteps but none existed—they had used the tree canopy, as a means of thoroughfare.

"We must get to the cave—I think they may try to make a sacrifice of her."

We ran back to the lake shore and moved toward the base of the mountain. I tried to avoid thinking about losing Carla, but the lack of any tangible evidence, besides her scream for help, had me at a disadvantage. I needed to trust my gut. The cave appeared to be a general meeting place for the island residence and it made sense they would make straight for it. If not, we would be at a loss as to where we might find her.

Several times, panic attacks came at me but I forced them from my mind and kept a steady gait behind Happydoo, who could easily outrun me.

"Go on ahead, Happydoo. I can't keep up with your pace. If you come across the forest dwellers and Mrs. Carla, you must assess the situation. If you believe her life to be in imminent danger, do what you must to save her."

The android acknowledged my instruction and surged ahead with the laser grasped tightly in its hand. I did my best but soon dropped far behind as the mountain loomed up ahead. I looked for the path we had previously used and could see the flattened bushes and foliage left in the wake of Happydoo's flight. The going became more difficult and I pinned my hopes on the android making it to the cave before the forest dwellers harmed Carla.

To avoid injury, I took care in the scramble up the steep slope but soon became conscious of the pain in my leg. The broken bone, although healed, still suffered tissue renewal and the constant action didn't help. With a final effort I made it up to the cave's entrance and stopped for a few seconds to regain my breath. The cave floor revealed a host of prints, many more than the day before—they had to be in here. The journey into the depths took some time with the slippery surface but eventually I could see a glow of light from the cavern and heard the sound of high pitched chants.

I could see Happydoo's form, in a crouch behind some large boulders adjacent to the cavern's entrance and pulled up behind him. The light came from a huge fire in the center, beside the altar. It struck me how much more advanced this group was. Charley and Co knew nothing of fire until we introduced them to it. My concern had been the effects on their natural evolutionary process.

Shadows from the large group of forest dwellers stretched outward to the walls of the cave —the humanoid-beasts jumped up and down in rhythm to a drum instrument somewhere in the background and appeared to be working themselves into a frenzy.

My eyes searched for Carla but she was nowhere to be seen. I didn't know what to make of it but the animals appeared to be in preparation— perhaps for a sacrifice to take place.

"Have you seen Mrs. Carla, at all?"

'Not yet, Master Beckett, but I'm sure she is here somewhere.'

"The altar is empty—a good sign," I said.

A large male walked up to the altar and held up its hands. I assumed it to be the leader and the group quietened down. A few words in the forest dweller language brought a measure of silence.

I turned my head toward Happydoo. "You should be able to translate the words from our colony's records of their speech."

'Indeed I can, Master Beckett. The male addressing the group is telling them to be quiet—I believe an announcement is forthcoming.'

The group, now reduced to a hush, waited for their leader to speak. After each sentence Happydoo translated in a soft tone.

'We have gathered to deal with the abomination in our midst. The sudden arrival of strangers in our land must be answered with force.'

He stopped for a moment as the group, in enthusiastic exuberance, shouted comments of acceptance before he continued on.

'We have the long white-hair in our clutches and it will be sacrificed to Bunduloo.'

Another frenzy of enthusiasm followed.

'We have discovered it to be a female of its species and due to its violent attitude we have fed it gundulla. It now sleeps peacefully and there is no need to fear it.'

Grunts of acknowledgment followed. From behind the altar two more forest dwellers appeared with an unresponsive body between them—Carla. I broke out in a copious sweat. If we did not intervene, the love of my life and reason for my continued existence would be taken from me. The sound of heartbeat thrashed in my ears. ∞∞

FOURTEEN

In the Nick of Time

"We have to intervene right now," I said. My voice brimmed with urgency. "Give me the laser— we'll stand up together. You step forward and tell the leader if he proceeds with the sacrifice, great harm will come to them. I will cover you."

The android handed me the weapon. It then stepped out from behind the boulder and with a loud voice, shouted out my message. The response from the group could not have been better. They all fell to the ground and turned their heads to look at Happydoo. The leader, immobilized by fear stood rooted to the spot, while the two behind him dropped Carla to the ground. She lay still, in a crumpled heap.

For good affect I pointed the laser at the walls behind them and shot off a beam, which sizzled and crackled, when it struck the rock. A large amount of soil and stone melted and crashed to the floor. The forest dwellers all cringed and huddled together in fear. They backed off, holding each other, cowered by the sight of Happydoo as he turned on the twin beams of dazzling light and swept the cavern from one side to the other. The translation facility, from our forest dweller education program and perfected by Laura Samuels, appeared work wonders on the locals.

"Address the leader. Tell him we mean them no harm and their god, Bunduloo, would not be happy with such a sacrifice."

By this time the creatures had moved to the back of the cavern and found themselves against the wall. We approached them with caution—the leader, and the only one still standing, acknowledged his understanding of Happydoo's words. He shook all over and averted his eyes from the android's powerful, spotlight beams.

I set the laser to stun anyone who tried to make a move toward us—Carla still lay unconscious on the ground. Happydoo pushed for an acknowledgement. The leader listened carefully and made several strangled grunts which I took to be his agreement. A possible reaction of fear, or in an act of sincerity he stretched out both hands, with open palms. To show good faith Happydoo did the same. I walked over to where Carla lay and knelt down by her inert body. I kept the laser in an offensive position in case the creatures reneged and felt her pulse—her cardiac rhythm appeared slow but steady. The forest dwellers must have access to some sort of natural drug, perhaps from a plant, which provided a state of comatose when consumed.

I shook Carla's shoulder and tried to wake her but she appeared to be in a deep sleep. Happy-doo came and stood next to me. The creatures all appeared to have gotten over the initial shock and crawled closer to inspect us but every time the android made a movement they cringed. I sat Carla up but her head lolled to one side. A few light slaps on the cheeks seemed to do nothing and I wondered if she would ever come round again.

The leader tentatively took a few steps toward me and extended his hand. Clutched in the fingers I could make out a cluster of what looked like flowers—he lifted them up to his broad nose, sniffed the flowers and extended the cluster to me.

'I think he is indicating for you to hold the flowers under Mrs. Carla's nose—maybe it's a type of reviving agent, Master Beckett.'

I took the plants from him and did as Happydoo suggested. A few moments later Carla's eyelids fluttered open and she stared at me. It took a further moment for her to register and she sat up with a sudden jerk.

"Take it easy, sweetheart. You've ingested some sort of drug to make you sleep."

"Oh God, Beckett. I thought I would never see you again," she mumbled.

"You're okay now, my love. We took a guess at where they were taking you and for what purpose."

"Where am I?" she asked. I could see by her eyes the effects of the drug still lingered.

"In the cavern—where we found the sacrifice."

Her eyes opened wide as comprehension returned. "Oh, no—please don't tell me I was about to become a sacrifice?"

I kissed her lips, thankful she showed no sign of harm. The leader stared transfixed at us, as though in a trance and in remembrance of our home dweller's psychology of behavior I walked up to him and stopped. He did not move and I detected the fear in his eyes. I reached out my hand in a slow, deliberate movement and placed it on his shoulder. In forest dweller terms this indicated an acceptance from a superior to an underling and the outcome of this act could go one of two ways. The leader might take umbrage at my forwardness in the show of superiority, or he might accept my position of strength, due to our ability to bring forth lightning and smoke.

He still made no movement either way, so I waited. At last he responded by placing his hand on my shoulder—it seems I had passed the test. He knelt and I placed my hand on his head. The group burst out in a jabber of noise which I took to be applause. I'm not sure whether they thought Happydoo and I to be gods or messengers, or perhaps some divine oracle. Disaster, however, appeared to have been averted. Carla stood a little unsteadily to her feet and leaned against Happydoo, who placed an arm around her for support.

The leader grinned and showed his front teeth. I let my hand slip off his shoulder and he turned to and jabbered away in a high-pitched voice. I asked Happydoo to interpret.

'He is saying the gods have come down from the great star to visit and they must make haste to prepare a great feast—it looks like we will be involved in the celebration, Master Beckett.'

The leader motioned toward the exit of the cavern and the group scurried out ahead of us. I put my arm around Carla and helped her through the cave to the entrance. The leader followed behind in a semi-crouch.

"Ask him what his name is."

The android turned and posed the question.

'His name, as far as I can make out is, Timokey, Master Beckett.'

"Tell him we would like to give him a new name. You can say it is the name his god, Bunduloo, calls him—Timmy."

The leader gave an enthusiastic shout of exuberance.

The trek down the mountain did not take us long. Timmy led us to a group of tall trees, similar to those Charley and Lucy lived in. We climbed up the vines to the first level where a platform construction awaited us. Carla, still a bit woozy from the drug effect needed help which both Happydoo and I provided, as we all climbed unsteadily to the first tier of their treetop abode. The establishment, more elaborate than our local forest dweller habitat, extended throughout a huge square area and I saw several ramps, which connected to higher tiers. The homes, all made from wood, clustered around the trunks of the supporting trees—some of the rooms appeared to be more than one story high.

Timmy spoke to Happydoo, who had now become our official go-between.

'He wants us to follow the female into the large building on the next level while he sees to the preparation of the feast, Master Beckett.'

"Is she his wife?" I asked.

'It would appear so, Master Beckett.'

I still could not help but experience concern for our safety and kept the laser at my side. We trooped up a connecting ramp toward a building which seemed much larger than the rest. The sudden change of events bothered me and I wondered at the genuineness of the attitude toward us— could it be a show, until we lulled ourselves into complacency? Time would tell.

Timmy's wife grinned at us and motioned everyone to be seated on the floor before she too disappeared. We sat and observed the skillfulness with which the hut's construction had been accomplished. These forest dwellers used the natural flora around them to create a beautiful assembly of treetop homes and I wished Charley could have been present to see it. I wondered about such a union. It seemed strange neither group ventured out onto the ocean's waters which teemed with aquatic life.

Timmy's wife returned with bowls of fruit and jugs of a strange colored liquid which I assumed to be a watered-down sap from one of the exotic jungle plants.

"Ask her what her name is."

Happydoo complied. 'My best translation would be 'Plishe', Master Beckett.'

Carla gave it a little thought and came up with a name. "We'll call her, Patty."

Happydoo made the exchange and the forest dweller knelt down for me to place my hand on her head.

"I'm sure they think we are gods," said Carla.

"Or the god's emissaries," I said. "Either way it benefits us until they can be better educated on the matter."

Timmy entered with a troop of dwellers behind him. They carried wooden plates and bowls of food—cooked meat and the edible bulbs of a plant. The servants appeared well disciplined and familiar with a routine of hospitality. Timmy and Patty set bowls before us and sat, one on each side. An awkward moment arose when Happydoo tried to explain he did not eat or drink and in the end, after several puzzled glances, he opted to tell them he suffered an allergy to certain foods and would eat later, when we returned to our home. I'm not sure if they understood but seemed content to let it go.

"The food is delicious," said Carla.

I agreed. "The taste of this sap drink is also good—something our group doesn't have."

"Don't drink too much of it," Carla warned. "It may be intoxicating."

One hour later we could eat and drink no more. Our hosts lay back, burped and farted loudly without any consideration for the three of us. We realized their customs differed from our local group but such goings on was an acceptable practice to Timmy and his dwellers. I knew Happydoo would be recording all of this and I would be able to entreat the others back home, of the circumstances and practices of this particular group.

A sudden shout, followed by a screech and a grunt emanated from outside, within the confines of the tree canopy. Timmy sprang to his feet and ran to the door. The noise continued and I guessed it might be some sort of altercation between a few of the resident creatures but our host shouted something at Happydoo and appeared perplexed. He rushed out the door and shouted commands to his group.

∞∞

FIFTEEN

The Habaka

"What's up Happydoo?" I asked.

'It would seem we are under attack from another group, Master Beckett. Timmy called them the 'Habaka'—he is rallying his people to fight them off.'

"Just our luck to end up in the middle of a forest dweller war," said Carla.

I stood and walked to the door. The uproar increased in volume but other than the shaking of branches, nothing could be seen. A forest dweller appeared out of the volume of leaves and sprang onto the platform close by the door, where I stood. I did not know if it belonged to Timmy's tribe or not but I soon deduced the answer to my own question—the creature almost fell off the platform when he saw me. I called for the laser, not sure what would happen next and Happydoo brought the weapon to me. The forest dweller appeared uncertain of the situation and shouted for reinforcements. Within a few moments half a dozen of them materialized through the leafy barrier and emboldened by numbers, charged at us.

I raised the laser and fired a shot at the feet of the lead creature. It stopped abruptly, with mouth agape at the smoke and sizzling timber. A quick glance at the laser's small control screen confirmed the setting to be in the kill-mode, so I retuned the charge back to stun-power. The last thing we wanted was to kill off the indigenous population. The forest dwellers turned, bailed off the platform into the branches and disappeared from view.

A short while later Patty jumped from a branch onto the platform and came into the room. I could see by her eyes all did not appear to be well. She spoke in a high pitched jabber—I turned to Happydoo for an explanation.

'The Habaka have taken Timmy prisoner, Master Beckett. Patty says they will kill him if we don't intervene. They usually have guards posted but because of our presence, everyone wanted to celebrate, so no one was at their post.'

"Does she know where the Habaka will take him?"

Happydoo posed the question and listened to Patty's answer.

'They will take him back to their camp for some sport before killing him, Master Beckett. She will ask her son to show us where it is but we must hurry.'

"You're not leaving me here, hon," said Carla. "I'm coming with you."

"The laser's charge is getting low," I said. "We only have enough power for one or two more shots. I will only use it if it's necessary. Happy-doo—I am going to set you into aggressive mode."

The Android turned and exposed his back for me to make the adjustment on his software.

Patty arrived with her young son in tow and jabbered excitedly to Happydoo.

'The boy will lead us, Master Beckett. We must be careful of the Prashta—a species of predator that attacks anything on sight. It lives in the deep forests, between us and the Habaka territory.'

"Ask her how the Habaka defend themselves against such a beast."

The android posed the question. *'They can only overcome a single Prashta with great numbers and the use of those spear-type weapons the guards have, Master Beckett.'*

"I will have to keep the laser for such an event, then. We will need to come up with something else against the Habaka."

The boy beckoned to us and we left the hut, climbed back down the vines to the ground and began to move through the forest on what appeared to be a game trail. The young boy moved in silence and kept looking back at us, while we brushed aside low branches and negotiated various obstacles. Our guide kept up a punishing stride which I assumed related more to urgency than his physical condition. After one hour of continuous exertion I stopped the youngster and told Happydoo to explain our need to rest.

He came to sit down beside Happydoo and a moment later I could see tears in his eyes.

"Tell the boy we will do everything to save his farther."

The boy lowered his head and continued to weep softly. I gave my water container to Carla who slugged down a few mouthfuls and we made the most of our short rest, by stretching out on the forest floor. The boy jumped up and jabbered to Happydoo in a sing-song lilt.

'We must keep going, Master Beckett. He says the Habaka are a ruthless race who will quickly dispose of his dad.'

I sighed and stood to my feet. "Come on, sweetheart. Let's get going."

Carla, fitter than I, grunted her despair but said nothing. We continued on with the path and after another half-hour came across an open field of grass, where the going became a lot easier.

The boy stopped unexpectedly, and dropped into a crouch. He motioned with his hand and signaled for us to do get down. I could not see the object of his concern but I heard its sudden growl—at the tree-line, on the edge of the field in the shade of a large bush, stood the most hideous of monsters. I could see why it took great numbers of forest dwellers to overcome one of these beasts.

The prashta stood at least seven feet tall. Its body, covered in scales and warts, stretched out behind the front legs and draped onto the ground.

It appeared to be sitting down with its rear legs folded beneath it. Vicious talons festooned the scaly front paws and everything about it oozed brute strength. The head, supported by a thick, short neck would have equaled the size of an ancient Earth elephant and when it opened its mouth, a jagged row of teeth gleamed in the sunlight. The dark brown scales looked almost impenetrable. When the prashta raised its tail I saw its most formidable weapon—a large bony structure, which I assumed, acted like a club. The creature stood up and I could see three sets of hind legs. I slipped the laser off safety and set the beam intensity to kill mode.

Time being of the essence, we could not afford to fight the beast off with the spear the boy carried. One strike of its tail would dislodge a head. I called to the boy and motioned for him to get behind me. The prashta moved deliberately toward us in a low crouch, with head lowered and teeth bared while it tried to frighten us with a low, rumbling growl. I stood my ground but the perspiration broke out on my brow. I needed to hit it right between the two large eyes and fry its brain.

The prashta entertained other ideas and turned its body to bring the tail into contention. The laser could incapacitate the movement of the tail but I did not know where to aim. With a movement that dazzled me it swung the tail around in an arc and I threw myself onto the ground. The bony club whistled over my shoulder and I shuddered to think what would have happened if it had hit the mark. The beast let out a loud bellow and repositioned its backside to deliver another blow. Rolling over in the grass to my left I came up, determined to fire off the laser at whatever target presented itself. The knee-high grass provided me with a bit of cover and for a moment the prashta hesitated. When I appeared on my knees with the laser pointed in the right direction, the flash of its eyes signaled it had pinpointed my position. The prashta swiveled the tail around for the death blow. Carla screamed for me to get out of the way but for some reason, I'm not sure why, I couldn't move.

At that moment the boy dashed out into the view of the prashta and threw the spear at its body. The point struck home on the body but made no impression other than a slight distraction. In the split-second of the creature's hesitation I took aim at the side of the large head and fired off a strong charge. The beam struck it below what I took to be an ear and the creature shuddered as a plume of smoke rose into the air.

The prashta roared and shook its head as if annoyed by a delinquent bug but it did not go down. I looked to see where Carla and Happydoo stood but they had already moved back several yards to a point where they could run into the forest if need be. The boy ran to join them and left me to face monster. The area of its head where the laser hit the mark, ejected puffs of smoke as the monster shook its head several times, in an effort to overcome the effect of high heat-energy destruction. The charge on the laser's power display showed four percent. The creature flopped around on wobbly legs and made a swivel action with its hips, to bring the tail around in my direction, again.

I ducked to avoid its final lunge as the club hurtled toward me. The bony projection caught my shoulder, to send me flying head over heels into the grass—the laser shot out of my hand. I landed on my back and for a moment everything went blank. Scenes of Earth, people whom I once knew, spoke with me and in turn I talked with Mickey, the Andromeda's master computer, about the Crustan attack—my uncle Sid reprimanded me for taking over the mining corporation and Dr. Abrams, of the Earth Relocation Project put her arm around my shoulders to comfort me.

I could feel the warmth of her body against mine—my eyes fluttered open and the visions disappeared—Carla held me in her arms and reality flooded back to my befuddled mind.

"What happened? Where's the prashta?"

"You're fine, hon. The beast knocked you down with its club-tail but I don't think you broke anything."

"Did it leave?" I asked. My mind cleared as strength flooded back into my body.

"It's dead—the laser strike did the work but it took a little while. Happydoo ran back and pulled you to safety. The prashta collapsed before it could get any closer to us."

I looked at the android. "It looks as though I owe you one again."

Happydoo performed his pirouette and foot-stomp routine.

'I am a pretty useful bucket of circuits and bolts, if I remember your usual response, Master Beckett.'

Despite the seriousness of our plight Carla and I managed to laugh at the android's comment.

The young boy jumped up and down to gain our attention. He jabbered and pointed toward the forest.

'He is reminding us of our mission, Master Beckett. We had better get moving.'

I agreed and stood up, a little unsteady on my feet. We forged on, past the dead carcass of the prashta, to reach the edge of forest where the going became tougher again. About twenty minutes later the boy stopped and motioned for us to get behind a bush. Ahead I could hear a commotion under the canopy of a group of trees—the sound of many voices, exuberant shouts and loud conversations. We moved forward to a vantage point where our presence would still remain undetected and peered through the thick foliage of the bushes.

∞∞

SIXTEEN

To the Rescue

A group of about twenty forest dwellers circled around a figure tied to a post and it became plain their taunts focused on one individual—Timmy. Trust up with vines he could do nothing but bow his head as stones rained down on his body and the occasional Habaka stepped up to slap, or punch him. I could see he faced impossible odds and the group seemed intent on bringing about his slow demise. I looked at Happydoo and motioned him to come closer.

"There isn't much Carla and I can do in this situation. We have one more shot with the laser, if I leave it on stun mode."

The android cocked its head. *'I'll take it from here, Master Beckett.'*

He stepped forward into the small clearing to assert a visible presence. The group, so intense, did not notice him at first but when the few on the fringe of the circle sensed his presence they screamed in high pitched forest dweller jabber. The rest of them stopped and stared at the android and backed away behind Timmy, to form a semi-circle.

Happydoo spoke in what appeared to be strong language and I assumed he had issued some sort of ultimatum. A large dweller moved forward a step and stared intently at us. By this time Carla, the boy and I had also stepped up behind the android. I held the laser at the ready—if they charged us we only had one chance.

Happydoo stated the same phrase at least three times and I wished I had possessed the good sense to bring the translator with us but Laura Samuels had needed it in the Dweller instruction classes. The Group leader seemed indignant at the intrusion and made several mock charges, to intimidate the android but Happydoo held his ground. The rest stood in silence and nobody took any further notice of Timmy, who still appeared to be aware of his surroundings.

After a lengthy exchange of sentences the leader grunted what I took to be an agreement.

"What's happening," I asked.

Happydoo turned his head. 'I have challenged this dweller to a competition—a fight, Master Beckett. I told him, if he wins he can do whatever he wants with us. If I beat him, he and his group must let us go.'

The leader turned to his followers and jabbered excitedly. They all responded with loud expressions of mirth and encouragement. I gathered he told them about the contest.

'You need to be ready with the laser in case I lose, Master Beckett. I have never taken on a forest dweller before so there is no way of knowing how strong they really are.'

"I trust your aggressive-protection mode will help you out. The last time it was used was when Lieutenant Sparkle needed your help against the Crustans."

'And still, I didn't take anyone on in hand to hand combat, Master Beckett. My program does allow for wrestling and boxing techniques, as these are considered sports.'

"Just pretend it's a sport and you'll do fine."

I recalled how people on Earth, valet owners, would set androids against other AI in competitions, for credit. My father, who owned Happydoo at the time believed it to be a barbaric practice, but now this same skill might save our lives.

The dweller moved toward Happydoo with intent. I could see by the gleam in his eyes he considered the contest to be a foregone conclusion. The android remained where he stood and waited for the leader to get closer. When three feet separated them the dweller stopped and they both stared at each other—a strange contrast. The dweller, shorter than his AI opponent possessed long arms, endowed with huge biceps and his hairy chest looked like an ancient beer barrel. I guessed him to be the leader of the group with the ability to inflict much pain on his subordinates should they disobey him. They slowly circled each other, the dweller with a grin and the android with no hint of any emotion on his synthetic facial features.

All of a sudden the dweller lunged at Happydoo, with both arms extended in an attempt to lock him in a bear-hug. The android slipped out of the grip with a quick twist of its body and moved toward the adversary's left. The dweller's grin disappeared perhaps in the realization his quarry possessed a few good moves. They continued to circle around each other for a few more seconds before the dweller tried again. This time he lunged in low, to attempt a tackle of the android's legs but to his astonishment Happydoo jumped about three feet into the air and avoided the move altogether. The dweller sprawled on the ground and to his embarrassment the group started to laugh at his ineptness. Happydoo kept circling and after a few more attempts to lay hands on him which all failed, the dweller looked confused and tired.

With sudden speed and agility the android made his move. To the forest dweller's absolute surprise Happydoo punched him on the side of the jawbone and knocked him onto the ground. The dweller roared in anger and sprang back onto his feet with one hand clutching the side of his face. He lunged without any regard for protection and missed the android's head with a vicious swing of his one fist. Happydoo side-stepped and caught him on the back of the head with a short, quick punch. The dweller looked a little dazed and swung around to face his adversary, who could not be found. The reason for the android's sudden disappearance lay in its extreme athletic abilities. Happydoo had jumped to a position behind his frustrated opponent.

The dweller looked around in mystification and the group pointed to where the android stood. He let out a growl of annoyance and swiveled around to face Happydoo again. This time the android taunted him and the outraged dweller rushed into grab it around the waist. Happydoo did not try to avoid him this time and I marveled at the strategy. The two went down in a tangle of legs and arms. The dweller, with his powerful body, made a quick move to get on top of the android and sit astride his abdomen. The huge biceps in the hairy arm flexed as he raised a fist, high above his Neanderthal-like head, to bring it smashing down on the android's face. The powerful brute could do an enormous amount of damage if the fist made contact, but Happydoo had other plans.

As the arm swiveled downward with the hairy fist aimed for a knockout blow, Happydoo twisted his frame and dislodged the dweller who fell onto his back in the short grass. The android moved like lightning and threw himself onto the hapless creature, to grab one long hairy arm with its bionic hands and stretch the arm over his one leg, which now lay across the creature's chest—I recognized the move as an ancient judo hold used by wrestlers many centuries ago. He applied pressure on the arm, against the normal bend of the elbow and pinned the dweller in a position from which it could not recover. The more the creature struggled, the more Happydoo applied pressure to the arm, to force the elbow against its normal bending motion.

The dweller frustrated and in obvious pain, refused at first to give up but the more pressure applied to the arm, the greater the sense of his defeat. The arm, now on the point where the elbow joint could not take any further pressure and on the verge of dislocation, brought final capitulation. After a few more moments he gave up. Happydoo held on for short while before letting go. He stood up and hovered over his conquered foe. The dweller could not look him in the eyes and turned its head to stare at the others. They all stood and gawked in a hush, at the quick disposal of their leader at the hands of the mysterious stranger. The android looked up at the crowd and raised his hand above his head in a symbol of victory and the group all looked at each other and chattered amongst themselves. The defeated foe lay still and stared at the ground in a state of complete exhaustion.

Happydoo addressed the group. They all appeared to understand what he asked for and two of them stepped up to Timmy, still tied to the post and released his bonds.

"Well, that seems to take care of it," I said.

Carla smiled. "I never knew Happydoo could even emulate such actions. It's amazing what he can achieve when in aggressive mode."

The two dwellers lifted Timmy onto his feet and dragged him over to us. His son ran forward with a squeal of delight and wrapped his arms around his dad. Happydoo leaned down to the leader, who still lay in a daze on the ground. The android reached down to grab the dweller's wrist and yanked him onto his feet. The leader looked sheepish and overwhelmed by his sudden defeat but made no move to retaliate in any way.

"It looks as though he is through," I said.

"I hope they understand we don't intend to harm them," said Carla.

"It may prove to be a good thing for our own protection. I think they are intrigued by us and won't try anything further."

I turned to Happydoo. "Any chance of brokering a peace between the two tribes?"

'I will be happy to try, Master Beckett.'

The android called the group to stand closer and addressed them on the issue. There were strange looks of puzzlement all round as they digested the words. The leader, having regained some of his composure joined in the conversation. He spoke in a subdued tone and it became evident his defeat placed him in awe of his opponent. Happydoo struck up a conversation with him and after several minutes they seemed to be as thick as thieves. Timmy became the sudden focus of attention and because of his prior association with us the group clapped him on the back as though they were all old friends.

"This seems to be going our way," I said.

Carla agreed. "I can hardly believe the change in their attitude."

"We need to press home the advantage of them working together and not against each other."

Happydoo must have overheard my conversation. 'I am suggesting that right at this moment, Master Beckett.'

The leader, now recovered from his ordeal, spoke to his group and they all danced around in jubilation.

'We have been invited to a feast, Master Beckett. We should acquiesce.'

An hour later we sat amongst a raucous party of forest dwellers, most of them high on the sap-type liquid Timmy and his family first introduced to us. I asked Happydoo to find out what the group called themselves. They were identical to Charley and Lucy. The android spoke to our host who answered with one word, which I recognized—Bashuku.

I turned to Carla. "These are obviously the family who left the main continent many years ago."

"That's wonderful, hon. I think Charley and Lucy will be ecstatic to learn they have relatives on this island."

We took conservative sips of the drink and kept our minds clear but the leader and several of his cronies became quite boisterous with each other. The treetop dwelling swayed back and forth to their antics, which caused me some concern, but things quietened down the more intoxicated they became. Timmy enjoyed his new found relationship with the Habaka and I saw our chances of an early exit dwindle away. To make matters worse the onset of darkness meant our return to Timmy's fold would be delayed until morning.

The leader stood and made some sort of libation to Happydoo who twisted his synthetic skin into a warm smile and the two of them exchanged forest dweller chatter.

'The leader says you can sleep in here tonight, Master Beckett—they will bring in furs for you to lie on. I have explained I will be leaving with immediate effect for personal reasons. My charge is running low and I need to get back to the antigrav. The boy will lead you back to Timmy's home.'

I understood the android's concerns. "That's fine. We'll leave at first light—perhaps you can inform Timmy's tribe that all is well."

'I am happy to do that, Master Beckett. You still have a very limited charge left on the laser but I doubt you will have any trouble getting back if you can avoid the prashta threat.'

"Perhaps the Habaka can send guards with us for the journey. It will also help them to further cement a good relationship with Timmy's folks."

Happydoo posed the question to the leader and confirmed the plan. Everyone left the room and all became quiet. A few moments later a dweller returned with a lot of furs for our comfort.

"I'm so tired, hon—I can hardly keep my eyes open," said Carla.

"Me too, sweetheart. Happydoo has given Timmy instructions for our return journey and asked him to join with me in standing guard tonight, in case our hosts have a sudden change of mind. We can take it in shifts."

My final words fell on deaf ears as Carla's breathing indicated sleep had already overtaken her. I nodded at Timmy and pointed to one of the furs on the floor and settled myself close to the entrance. Despite my resolve to be on guard, within minutes sleep took me to the land of nod.

∞∞

SEVENTEEN

One Big Family

The rays of 51 Pegasus streamed in through the doorway, onto my face. I awoke with a start and for a moment confusion reigned in my mind. Timmy and Carla lay stretched out on their respective furs, both still asleep. I stretched my limbs, arched my back and emitted a cavernous yawn, not too proud of the fact I had lost the battle to stay awake the previous evening. Without anyone to wake Timmy for his shift he continued to sleep and I felt bad about my failure, however, all seemed in order.

Outside the hut I walked around the limited area provided by the platform and listened for sounds of the forest dwellers. The dense leaf coverage made it difficult to see the surroundings but I heard a baby cry somewhere in the adjacent canopy. The noise of other dwellers about to start their morning rituals, floated through the treetops. I heard a noise behind me and Timmy appeared, wiping sleep from his eyes. He grinned and made a grunting sound. I guessed it to be the equivalent of a good morning greeting. Any communication between us would, without Happydoo, have to be done with signs. Carla also appeared in the door-way and smiled.

"Good morning my love, it looks like a love-ly day." She said.

I agreed. "As nice as it is here I'm longing to get back to our home."

Our host appeared through the leaves, his three fingered hand with its thumb clutched on a vine for balance, while he stepped onto our plat-form from an adjacent branch. Timmy greeted him and the two did the typical forest dweller embrace. The friendship still seemed on good terms, a mira-cle considering the Habaka's intent of the previous day, before our intervention. Another two females followed in his wake. Both clutched bowls of fruit and barakis milk.

After a good breakfast our host indicated for us to descend the vines to the ground for our jour-ney. Four Habaka awaited us, each with the typical spear and we bade the group of dwellers goodbye. Timmy and his son embraced several of the group before leaving and much excited jabber followed until we waved goodbye and disappeared into the trees.

The trek back to the Bashuku camp took several hours. Fortunately, no prashta threat availed itself and we arrived at Timmy's home in good spirits. Timmy's family rushed down the vines from the canopy to greet us and a joyous re-union followed, with much excited jabber and screeching. The good news, shared by Happydoo on his way to our camp obviously prepared them for our homecoming and signs of a great celebration appeared to be underway. Carla and I wanted to leave for our camp on the lake shore but the Bashuku restrained us with signs and gesticulations. It appeared they wanted us to be their honored guests for a short while longer.

"I hope Happydoo will return to the Bashuku camp when his charge is done," I said.

Carla laughed. "I'm sure he realizes how awkward it is for us without a translator. We should have determined to learn their language a long time ago."

"You're right, sweetheart. Having them learn our language is easy for us but difficult for them."

We ascended the vines into the treetop and clambered onto the platform. The hut contained bowls of food, barakis milk and the intoxicating sap, all in honor of our presence.

As we sat down on the floor a familiar voice sounded in our ears. 'I trust your journey was without incident, Master Beckett?'

Happydoo looked in at us from the hut entrance.

"We're relieved to be back and to have someone translate for us—I can't think of enough appropriate signs to convey my intensions," I said.

Much to the astonishment of the dwellers, the android did his pirouette and foot-stomp routine. He explained the antic to them and they relaxed. Lengthy speeches followed extolling our virtues on the rescue of Timmy. The potential peace between the Habaka and the Bashuku took a further turn with a ceremony of honorary tribe induction of the four Habaka guards. I could feel my senses start to swirl a little from the sap which drew a concerned frown from Carla. After several hours, spurred on by the failing light, I told Happydoo to announce our departure for the camp. The party did not end there, however—the entire camp accompanied us. On arrival, they stood around the antigrav in wonderment while Happydoo and I folded up the yurt.

Happydoo told them we would return in a few weeks with Lucy and Charley—if we could convince the couple to fly in the antigrav. It appeared almost certain the two tribes shared a common ancestor. After lengthy goodbyes we departed the island and made for the mainland.

*

Our arrival back at the village brought everyone to the antigrav, as it landed in the quadrangle in front of the command pod. My dad and Freda, accompanied by Rebecca and her husband, Philip, greeted us with broad smiles and hugs. Our sojourn on the Habaka's island had lasted for five days but it seemed a lot longer. Hera-soter now replaced the sense of home which our mother planet, Earth, had always meant for us. It occurred to me we should begin to name the islands and continents within our capability of exploration, thanks to the Prime Endeavor's antigrav.

The continent on which we originally landed already carried the name of Bashukuland, in honor of Charley and Lucy's tribe. Our people's exploits covered all the places on the continent and each had been given a name. The area around our village plus the adjacent lake, received the name of Abrams, in honor of the Relocation Director, Dr. Abrams. Rebecca shared that Dr. Abrams would be resigning her position to participate in the next mission to Hera-soter.

The Andromeda, now a museum continued to orbit the planet. Mickey originally set up a geosynchronous orbit but I recently changed it to a normal orbit with the idea of using the Andromeda as a satellite for monitoring the entire planet plus the solar system.

My dad embraced me in a strong grip. "How was your trip?"

"Extremely interesting," I said.

Carla giggled. "I would say it was more than interesting."

We spent the following day with the Establishment Committee and told them of our experiences. Carla suggested we call the island, Habaka. We shared the plan to reunite Charley and Lucy with their cousins.

"Your discovery means the possibility of other tribes on the rest of the land masses," said Rebecca.

"Are we going to reeducate these people," asked Philip.

"We have done it for the Bashuku—so it makes sense to continue their upgrade to eventually reach our status," said Carla.

"It has raised some ethical problems amongst some of our evolutionary scientists," said Rebecca. "They argue it would be detrimental to skip all the relevant phases of the animal's evolutionary process."

"It's a fair observation. I can understand their concern, however, the Bashuku have well-developed frontal lobes and appear ready to advance. They are not like the early hominins of Earth, whose brains were about the size of an orange."

My dad chipped in. "I think they should be allowed to advance at their own pace. We make instruction available and if they want to advance they should be allowed to."

"It may not be that simple, Padraig," said Rebecca. "There are many aspects of development to consider. We have no idea as to their emotional stability in advanced situations. I think much research must be done before we take them out of the trees."

I needed to curtail the discussion before an argument developed. None of us had given much thought, as to how far the Bashuku's education should be taken.

"I suggest we set up a panel of scientists to do the relevant research and tests. The Bashuku are such a willing species and will comply with whatever we ask. We know they are capable of learning the language but none of them have shown any interest in living amongst us on the ground," I said.

Everyone agreed and we moved onto more productive subjects. We discussed the need to establish a currency for business and set up a more aggressive economy. With the arrival of Rebecca and her people, production and consumption had escalated—with it came the need for a more sustainable economic system.

"As chairmen I suggest we set up a commission group to plan out a system of credits for accomplished work. We have Mickey to create the framework and monitor everyone's personal input to the Hera-sotern economy. We also have our Earth history, of all the snags and pitfalls of such an arrangement."

All agreed to the suggestion and Mickey took the minutes for later orchestration of an economic model for the new structure. The final item on the agenda encouraged the newer members of the committee to ask questions regarding the way things were going. One of Rebecca's people stood up and cleared his throat.

"My name is Benjamin Sprack and I am an expert in Political Government Systems. I want to say how wonderful it is for us to be so well received by the original group. I also applaud the original committee for the way things have been setup here, on Hera-soter. I must, however, throw a fish back into the water and I would like to explain why."

∞∞

EIGHTEEN

Dr. Sprack

I looked at Rebecca and Philip. They swiveled their eyes to look at each other and I took it they found Sprack's intrusion to be unwelcomed.

Sprack glanced around at the faces before him and took a moment to assess his reception. My mind surged back to my project training and the protocol Dr. Abrams laid down for the establishment of the early settlers on Hera-soter. The government model we employed did not reflect all the tenets of the original protocol. The reason for this stemmed from differences in the terrain, the climate and available resources. We also included the association of another species, the forest dwellers, into our daily decisions. A further consideration rested in the fact of there being only a few willing minds available to deal with everyone else's problems, plus their own. Protocols for these could not be established by forethought but by actual on-site experience. I made no comment and waited for him to continue.

"To start with, we have too few members of the total, making the most important decisions for the colony. Another problem I see is the reliance on android's and the master computer, Mickey, for answers which humans should be responsible for."

I felt a knot developing in my stomach and cut in to his speech. "With all due respect for your expertise in the area of local governance, Dr. Sprack, the establishment of any colony in the outer reaches of space requires more than laid down protocols—particularly by people who have never been into space. While I respect the tide of human knowledge, our computer-driven intelligence provides us with accurate information, unfettered by human assumptions."

Sprack did not look phased. "I understand your position Dr. Conroy. You have needed to rely on these machines because you were under a significant alien threat. Computers, with their highly intelligent processors need to be respected when the chips are down, but in times of normalcy, human perspective is much better."

I countered his argument. "These are extremely advanced and sophisticated AI's, who often do a much better job of providing solutions than the fickle human mind. It's a case of judging the outcomes."

Lieutenant Sparkle, the appointed representative for the people on our mission stood to his feet. "May I say something, Mr. Chairman?"

"Go ahead, Sparkle," I answered.

Sparkle turned to address Sprack, who looked down his long, pointed nose at the android.

'I'm not sure if you are aware of the Diamond 1000 processor, Dr. Sprack.'

Sprack nodded. "I'm aware of its capabilities."

The lieutenant's digital purr softened to imitate human expression. 'What you may not be aware of is the confluence of emotional reaction with the almost infinite database of statistics and facts to create a process of reasoning, which takes place in the face of any circumstance. What I am saying, Dr. Sprack, is that the Diamond 1000 creates a reasoning process similar to that of a human mind—with its accompanying emotions. This is a quantum entangled process which goes beyond the standard model of quantum mechanics.'

Sprack absorbed the information and then raised his chin. "I did know about the Diamond 1000 processors capabilities, Lieutenant. It is the reason Dr. Abrams appointed you as a representative of the people on Dr. Conroy's mission. Technology still does not completely emulate the human mind and in my thinking does not replace the intuition aspect humans are capable of."

I stepped in. "I don't think we can resolve your dilemma in this meeting, Dr. Sprack."

I turned to the main console. "Mickey? Can you please schedule a meeting in a week's time, to talk about this aspect of government?"

'It is done, Boss,' said Mickey.

I thanked everyone for their input and closed the meeting. After the committee members left Rebecca and Philip came to me.

"I apologize for Dr. Sprack, Beckett. He tried several times to come between the people and our leadership during our flight. He is the reason why we have no androids on the mission and our master computer is relegated to matters of the starship only," said Rebecca.

"It's just as well you didn't run into the type of trouble we did—it was the AI's who saved us. No human could have possibly achieved what they did for the good of the mission," I responded.

"It must be understood why he holds this view," said Philip.

"I'm listening," I said.

"He's entire family was wiped out by a renegade android, whose programs had been purposely adjusted to do so. They discovered it to be someone working in the android upgrade center with a grudge against his family."

I understood the position but it did not explain Sprack's total negativity regarding artificial intelligence—ultimately, people were responsible for his family's demise.

"Our lives are so intertwined with AI it is difficult to imagine carrying on without them," I said.

"Unfortunately, Sprack has voiced his opinions time and time again. No doubt he'll try to influence the colony's original settlers and I'm not quite sure whether the correct thing to do is ignore the issue," said Philip.

I wanted to get back to Carla, who did not attend the meeting due to a fever. She and Happy-doo undertook the short trek to the Prime Endeavor in order to make use of the onboard medical imaging process. Both of us maintained good health until a few day prior, when she started to feel queasy in the mornings with occasional dizzy spells. I had my suspicions but thought it best she be checked out by the diagnostic equipment.

"We can talk about Sprack later. I want to hear what Carla has to say."

They both agreed and asked for an update on her condition as soon as I knew. Lieutenant Sparkle hovered in the background and I knew he wanted to address the issue about Sprack's anti-android sentiments. I turned to him. "Can we talk about the issue later, Sparkle—I need to determine my wife's condition."

'Give Mrs. Conroy my best, Mr. Chairman.'

When I entered the front door of our home Carla sat on the settee with a grin on her face.

"So, what's the news," I asked.

"I'm pregnant."

Although I suspected the possibility it still came as a shock to my system—a wonderful surprise of gargantuan proportions.

"That is wonderful news, sweetheart. Is it too early to tell the gender?" I asked.

"The doctor in charge of the clinic says it's a boy."

"I hold no preferences but a son would be great for a start. We have to tell everyone and celebrate the good news."

I could not stop grinning for the rest of the day. By late afternoon the entire village knew of the pending birth and congratulations flooded our omninet mailbox. Well-wishers came in droves to our door and we spent most of our evening entertaining our many friends. My dad, overjoyed at the prospect of being a grandfather, brought out a bottle of Supernova whisky, to toast the prospect of new-born life and I suffered the consequences come the next morning.

A week later I still could not stop talking about my son. Some darker moments overcame me when I thought of my own childhood. My dad, an absent parent due to the nature of his work, featured highly in my early rebellion of his negligent oversight and I found myself thinking negatively toward him at times. Carla picked up on my brooding and knew exactly what plagued me.

"You have to remember one thing, Beckett—your father became a victim of his passion and drive to help the human race survive a negative birth rate. He provided you with the means to resolve the problem, which you did. You forgave him many years ago, so don't allow the ghosts of the past to return and ruin the future."

I considered the comment. "You are absolutely right sweetheart. I let go of my rage and promised myself it would never return—but now I am the one to become a father and I don't want to make the same mistake my dad did. I guess I allowed the news to drag me in the opposite direction. If you ever see me become too absorbed with my work, please hit me over the head."

She laughed. "I will. You need to go and give your dad a hug—make sure he doesn't ever become the object of your wrath again. What is done is done and you need to consider the hatchet buried."

*

Lieutenant Sparkle knocked on the command pod's door and asked permission to enter. Reports regarding the latest details of a mining endeavor on Habaka Island consumed my attention. A prospecting team's discovery of a rock-element containing a radioactive isotope brought much needed hope for our power source requirements.

"What's up, Lieutenant?"

'Have you seen Happydoo, Sir?'

"No, actually I haven't seen him for at least two days—he might be visiting the forest dwellers."

'I've checked with Charley and Lucy but they haven't seen him either, Mr. Chairman.'

"It's unusual for him not to be around the village. I will call Mrs. Conroy and ask her if she knows where he might be. Is there any particular reason why you need to see him, Lieutenant?

'We have been engaged in the setup of a work-plan in conjunction with Chief Spanner, for the manufacture of two more androids as per your requirements, Mr. Chairman.'

I called Carla on the omninet; she did not know where the android was. Happydoo's role, apart from being my valet, embraced the routines of security inspections and monitoring of the agricultural progress of our many crops. Our farm, situated on a section of fertile land between the village and the mountain, required regular observation, due to small animal and pestilent scavengers. Dozens of small rodent-like creatures called "skenka" continuously raided the genetically altered fruit and vegetable plants, grown from Earth seedlings.

"You had better see if you can find him, Sparkle. He might be out on the farm."

'I will take Chief Spanner with me. I'm sure we will find him, Mr. Chairman.'

"Put your cameras on holographic broadcast so I can I see where you go and what you find."

The android left and I returned to my reports. Ten minutes later a hologram sparked on the holo-platform and I cast my eye in its direction from time to time. The two androids marched in a single file along the path toward the farm and I could see the entire landscape before them. The trudge of their feet carried a rhythmic sound, like two soldiers on a route march.

The reports further absorbed my attention and after some time, when the two marchers came to a sudden stop, it jolted me back to their mission. The Lieutenant's eye-cameras focused on a section of ground upon which a body lay—the inert form of Happydoo.

∞∞

NINETEEN

Android-phobia

I jumped up from my seat and approached the holo-platform. The angles at which my valet's legs and arms where spread-eagled suggested an accident of some sort. I stared with trepidation and astonishment.

Sparkle's voice sounded calm and emotionless. *'Are you getting this, Mr. Chairman?'*

"I see it. What has happened?"

'It appears your valet has been hit in the back of the head with a laser charge. The cranium has suffered severe damage, Mr. Chairman.'

"Is there any sign of a weapon or anything suspicious?"

'No sign of a weapon, Mr. Chairman, but I did find this—'

I squinted into the hologram as the Lieutenant held a peaked cap up to his eyes so the cameras could focus on it. He turned the cap to show a logo and I recognized it immediately—the starship, Prime Endeavor, emblem.

"How bad is the damage, Lieutenant?"

'It's bad, Sir. A high intensity laser charge aimed at maximum damage, from behind. Happydoo didn't stand a chance.'

I felt a sudden grief at the loss of my valet. One-hundred and fifty years spanned its connection with my family. Tears welled up in my eyes as the thought of life without him impacted me. Then I remembered. Still aboard the Andromeda, the processor programs for all three androids, lay locked in a special vault. Somehow, in transition from the ship to the planet, this important aspect had been forgotten. Years before the Relocation Project came into being, after the almost complete destruction of Happydoo by the EIA at the time Carla and I fought to retain the research information of my dad's longevity breakthrough, a backup of the android's processor had been made. The idea, the brainchild of a friend who worked in Central's Android Reconstruction factory, would now stand me in good stead.

Without the backup Happydoo's unique personality would be lost. The alternatives rested in a completely new android for a valet, or dispensing with the service altogether. I could not bear the thought of the latter. The engineers, resident on the Prime Endeavor could easily replace the android's processor unit and Happydoo's unique cranial features, with the starship's on-board printer. My greatest concern, however, lay in getting to the Andromeda. The PE's antigrav required an atmosphere to operate in and could not be used for any form of space travel.

I called Rebecca on the omninet. "Does the PE have a space vehicle I could use for a trip to the Andromeda?"

"No, but we have EEP's that could be converted for a short trip. I would have to ask our engineers if a takeoff from the planet is a possibility. As you know EEPs are meant for emergency escape in space. Why do you ask?"

I explained the situation. "I need to talk with you and Philip about my suspicions." I did not mention the cap Sparkle found close by the crime scene.

"That's awful, Beckett. I'll contact our chief engineer and find out what we can do with the use of an EEP."

I switched back to my contact with the lieutenant. "Take Happydoo to the Prime Endeavor's maintenance section and speak to the chief in charge of their workshop. Tell him we'll supply the program details if he can provide an upgraded processor and repair the damage. When you return to the village, come straight to the command pod."

'Chief Spanner and I will leave for the PE right away, Mr. Chairman.'

"Be on the lookout for anything, Sparkle. It looks as though someone wants to decimate our android compliment and I think I know who."

I left the pod and returned home to Carla. My sudden grief morphed into anger at the person I suspected to be behind the attack—Dr. Sprack. The peaked cap with the PE emblem would not be enough to prove his guilt but no one else had expressed any reservations about the androids in our midst. I needed to get to the bottom of the matter and deal with it.

Carla's forehead creased in a frown. "Someone tried to eliminate Happydoo? Who do you think it might be?"

"I can only think of Dr. Sprack's little speech at the committee meeting. I can't think of anyone else who has ever said anything bad about our androids."

"What are you going to do?"

"I am meeting with Rebecca and Philip to discuss a possible game plan. They should be here any minute."

The knock on the door came simultaneously. Rebecca and Philip walked into the living room and sat down. We talked briefly about Carla's condition and the baby, before the topic of Sprack came up.

Rebecca sat up straight and for Carla's benefit shared Sprack's story with us.

"I think he managed to sway a few people while on the journey. We need to test the sentiment somehow to see what sort of influence he's generated. Our project management rejected the use of androids and that came from higher up than Dr. Abrams."

Her comment tweaked my interest. "Do you know who might have been involved in that decision?"

Philip answered my question. "I believe one of the anti-droid advocates in The Administration. She was involved in the setup of the first project and consequent refurbish of the Andromeda."

The hair on the back of my neck stood up. "Do you know what section she was involved with?"

"I believe it was the program upgrade for your Master Computer—Mickey."

Things fell into place with sudden alacrity. "I don't doubt a man by the name of Colin Pearson worked under her at the time."

I regurgitated the facts of our near demise by the hand of Gary Pearson the Andromeda's XO, in the attempt to remove me from leadership. "I think Dr. Sprack's agenda might be greater than eliminating our androids."

We sat in silence and stared at each other as the truth sank in, before Carla made a statement.

"We don't want to go through this again. I suggest our security get involved before anything more sinister than an attack on one of the androids, goes down. I will speak to Mike Hunter."

My protective streak jumped into the lineup of suggestions. "I don't want you involved, sweetheart. You now have a new responsibility—our child and your health. I will take care of it."

She shot me a wistful look. "You have so much on your plate as it is, Beckett. I will speak to Mike and then leave it with him—I promise."

I got that look again and backed off. "That's fine my love, but after you have spoken to him you must leave it with us."

She acquiesced but I could see it did not sit well with her.

Rebecca and Philip stood to leave. "You should get your rest now, Carla and please don't worry. We'll figure something out. Sprack is an insidious type of person and should not be underestimated."

Carla shrugged. "I have had some experience with this type of situation and Sprack will soon find out what he's up against," she said.

I jumped in to clear up what she alluded to. "Carla used to work for the NWEIA before we became involved. She understands security issues quite well."

Rebecca smiled. "All the same—she should limit her involvement and take care of herself and the baby. Sprack arrived on Hera-soter through our mission and we'll take care of it."

"Sprack is now our problem too as he is a part of the local community—we all have a responsibility," I concluded.

Philip and Rebecca left after giving Carla a hug. I knew nothing would prevent her involvement in getting to the bottom of the situation. The look on her face told its own tale.

A knock on the door revealed the presence of Lieutenant Sparkle and Chief Spanner.

'We have done as you asked," said the android. *'Happydoo is now with chief engineer Edwards, who will start the refurbishing process.'*

We did not know how far Sprack's influence extended. What if this engineer fell within Sprack's anti-android community? I thanked Sparkle and told him we would make preparation to get to the Andromeda for the android's backup vials.

'I would like to be considered for that duty, Sir. I doubt if we could trust any of the PE's personnel.'

"I will arrange it," I said.

*

Rebecca confirmed the PE's chief engineer to be one of her oldest friends and longtime colleagues.

"Happydoo will be completely safe with Edwards. He's been involved with android manufacture and improvement programs for years and it is one of his specialties."

"What does he say about the possible use of an EEP for transport to the Andromeda?" I asked.

"He says it is entirely possible and has started to work on the project for the provision of a take-off control system. If it doesn't work we'll use the Prime Endeavor to make the trip."

I breathed easier and thanked her for the offer. I knew it would take several days to prepare the PE for such a trip, which might also endanger the technical resources we now relied upon for the community. The use of an EEP would be much easier. Carla contacted Mike Hunter, head of the village security to initiate a discussion about our problem with Sprack. I decided to leave it to her and walked back to the command pod.

An hour later, Chief Edwards from the PE's maintenance called me. "We have worked out a system to assist and control an EEP takeoff, Mr. Chairman. It should handle the atmosphere with ease. It will be ready for flight tomorrow."

"Wonderful news, Chief. I'll send Lieutenant Sparkle along first thing in the morning."

∞∞

TWENTY

Techno-Resuscitation

The flight to the Andromeda went off without a hitch. Lieutenant Sparkle found the program vials in the vault and the entire trip took about half an hour. Chief Edwards removed Happydoo's damaged computer and replaced it with the latest technology, a D-2000, taken from one of the PE's three backup systems. The processor, an improved version of the D-1000, would endow Happydoo with greater abilities than Sparkle, so I took the liberty and asked Edwards to upgrade the lieutenant's software at the same time.

Mike Hunter, briefed by Carla on the Sprack affair, deployed his agents to infiltrate general village conversations to broach the subject of androids and their usefulness to our society. It appeared most people were in favor of android involvement but several, mostly from Rebecca's group, expressed some reservations. The specific objections paralleled the sentiments of Dr. Sprack and it soon became evident most of the dissenters fell under his influence. Carla wanted to have Sprack brought in and questioned, but I refused.

"We can't prove anything yet, sweetheart. We need more evidence of his collusion with the likes of Gary Pearson and the plot to have us eliminated."

"I think we could make a case with what we already know, hon. I don't see the sense of waiting until he commits another crime."

I needed to be astute in my reasoning. "Sweetheart—I understand your objections, but we need to prove Sprack's complicity in the crime against Happydoo before we can proceed to bring the full extent of our law against him. If we try to prosecute him on android intolerance a court of law would throw it out on insufficient evidence. At best they will tell him to refrain from comments on the subject. We must work within the framework of our own legal system."

"What about Happydoo? Are not he, Sparkle and Chief Spanner at risk?" said Carla.

"They are at a certain amount of risk. Happydoo has been upgraded to the latest Diamond technology and I've asked Chief Edwards to do the same for Sparkle. Chief Spanner is at much less risk because he's not out of the village's industrial section for any length of time. The D2000 has major detection abilities and the androids are aware of the danger."

"Okay, so we wait," she said. "But Mike will continue his surveillance until we get something of importance."

"I agree. I'm sure something will crop up soon."

We slept on it and the following morning Chief Edwards called me on the omninet. "Your two androids are ready to be recommissioned. There should be no change to their respective personalities and the reprogramming will provide them with improved abilities in aggressive mode. I am going to give you the codes and I suggest you commit them to memory."

"Thanks Chief. Will you send my valet to the command pod when it's done?"

Two hours later I heard a familiar shuffle at the pod door and looked up to see Happydoo.

"Welcome home, my friend," I said. His reconstruction, considering the amount of damage done to his cranium, showed an expert hand at work.

'I am happy to be back in the land of cyber-reality, Master Beckett.'

"You certainly are a tough old bucket of bolts," I said.

This sparked off the routine and I knew things were back to normal.

'Lieutenant Sparkle and Chief Spanner shared the details of my close demise, Master Beckett. I never detected the presence of any person near me, despite my sensors.'

"We have our suspicions about your assailant—you were close to another heat source which hid the criminal's position."

'It will not happen again, Master Beckett. I am now the proud recipient of a D2000 processor.'

I swore I could detect an element of pride in the android's voice. "I believe so, my friend. Use it wisely—we need to unveil your assailant's future intensions."

I shared the news of Dr. Sprack's connection to the plot in regards to the rebellion on the Andromeda. The android's eyes oscillated a brilliant blue as it processed the information and cocked its head in typical android fashion.

'That is very interesting, Master Beckett. I have a plan.'

"What do you propose," I asked.

'I believe Dr. Sprack holds a class for young people who are interested in Government systems, Master Beckett. I have a young human friend who I can ask to attend this meeting and see where it leads. I think the doctor must be planning something. Maybe my plant will be able to get on the inside by winning his confidence.'

"Great idea, Happydoo. I'll let Mrs. Carla and Mike Hunter know what we intend to do."

The foot-stomp routine followed. It pleased me greatly to have my valet back again. The suggestion to infiltrate Sprack's inner circle resonated with the need to do be proactive.

*

A week later Happydoo brought us some good news.

'My contact reports she is now attending Dr. Sprack's meeting on Government Systems, Master Beckett. Sprack intends to start a university-level course for young students who are interested.'

"He hasn't bothered to clear it with the Establishment Committee," I declared.

The Establishment Committee vetted all the educational aspirations of the colony and did not take kindly to anyone starting random courses without consultation. We did not doubt his ability to establish such a venture but it needed to fit the needs of the community. I suspected the classes would be a vehicle with which he could pedal his poison.

"We won't say anything to the Committee about it at this time. We'll let him continue with the hope of catching him out."

'Dr. Sprack has suggested to my friend she attend a cafteen meeting in the dungeon tonight, Master Beckett. I think this will be the beginning of indoctrination or a suggestion of a drive to change the way the people are governed.'

"I would be very interested to hear what the outcome of that would be," I said.

The Dungeon, a popular venue for people who enjoyed a good conversation at the end of the work day offered cafteen, light snacks and music. I thought of paying it a visit but decided my presence might be a deterrent for the likes of Sprack. The best course of action would be to keep a low profile on the issue and wait for something concrete to happen.

"Have you tested out your new capabilities?" I asked.

'I have tried the new danger detection potential—it is extraordinary, Master Beckett. I believe the program also allows for an aggression beyond my civil scope but if you care to assess the range you may slip me into the relevant mode and we can see how it works.'

"Let's hope the need for those extra powers never arises but it's a comfort to know there are two of you who can perform at the military level."

The android gave one of its customary chuckles. 'It's also a consolation for me to know that as long as a vial with all my programming exists I can never die, Master Beckett.'

This time I laughed. "It's an interesting concept."

My father had actually placed humans in the same boat with his success at consciousness transfer. The Relocation project made use of it for our hibernation over the long haul from Earth to Hera-soter. The Administration back on Earth, however, had set up a moratorium to prevent use of the breakthrough.

'I can understand the human sentiment of longevity, Master Beckett. It is a great moral argument which fortunately does not affect the restoration of androids.'

"Yet, Artificial Intelligence appears as much a life to me as human life—I believe androids have reached a gray area where we aren't exactly sure what happens in the quantum entanglement process, which mimics human behavior. You appear to have genuine feelings and emotions but don't let it go to your head—you are still my bucket of bolts and electrical circuits."

The android slapped his thigh and threw in a new chuckle, followed by the classic routine. I felt a genuine affection for it. "When will you speak to your contact again?"

'When she returns from the meeting with Dr. Sprack, Master Beckett. I will let you know.'

Ten minutes after Happydoo left the pod Lieutenant Sparkle strolled in.

"Feeling rejuvenated, Sparkle?"

'The Diamond 2000 is magic, Mr. Chairman.'

"I believe so. Happydoo is in the clouds about it."

'I thought I would share something important, Sir. With the D2000 processor there is no need for a recharge from an electrical source anymore due to the addition of a nuclear battery, which the Relocation Project engineers invented in conjunction with the military. Chief Edwards received the details on the day the PE left for deep space.'

"That's a great advancement," I said.

'It is, Mr. Chairman and I'm glad to say the upgrade saved me from possible destruction. On arrival back at the village I dropped into our charge-depot and started to dismantle my charge-up system when I discovered the attachment of a small incendiary device. Had I connected to the charge input, the entire pod would have been blasted to oblivion.'

I stared at him in consternation. "It looks as though our enemy is hard at work. You had better inform Chief Spanner."

∞∞

TWENTY-ONE

Keeping an Eye on Sprack

The following day Happydoo reported on the event at the Dungeon. Sprack's involvement appeared more far-reaching than mere destruction of the androids. Our spy, a young girl, alluded to certain insinuations Sprack made against the Establishment Committee's control of the colony. He felt a president should be elected and a formal political process be introduced for the good of everyone. I knew Dr. Abrams, of the Relocation Project must have laid out the steps of colony establishment before the PE's departure, but Sprack obviously disagreed with her establishment premise. I recalled a movement while on our mission's early training, of a group that agitated for a return to the failed democratic process of the twentieth and twenty-first centuries.

The Administration's reaction to the group bordered on suspicion of a conspiracy and the leaders found themselves under critical scrutiny, but nothing ever came of it. The New World Earth system of government, a group of prominent leaders, chosen by their respective continental governments, ran the Earth's global affairs with the help of a dynamic super computer called 'Central.' Fifty percent of these chosen delegates were androids. The Relocation Project's plan for government, on our new planet started with a committee to be elected by the Andromeda's mission principles—Carla and I. The future would develop along similar lines of the New World Earth, in time. Mickey now operated in conjunction with the newer PE's processor, to kept the colony's business world on track.

"What did our spy make of Sprack," I asked.

'She believes he will try to influence more and more people to his way of thinking and then confront the Committee with an ultimatum, Master Beckett. This characterized his general conversation with the ten people who met with him last night.'

"Please convey our gratitude to her for the report and tell her to be careful. Only a few of us are aware that something is afoot and we need to keep it that way—she needs to be discreet and not share her findings with anyone other than you."

*

Six weeks later the reports from our spy suggested Sprack's plan to cause trouble had gained some momentum. His contingent of sympathizers, about two-hundred and fifty people, now met under the guise of an agricultural venture which he cleverly cleared with the Establishment Committee. Only the three androids, Carla, Rebecca, Philip and I, knew the real intention of his group. They met out in the farm on the second afternoon of every week, to plan their mission. When Chief Edwards came to Rebecca with a suspicion of a cover up in the PE's armory, detected by one of his ensigns, we knew things were on the move. The ensign's superior, a known Sprack collaborator moved fifty laser-rifles from the gun-vault for maintenance which would not be out of the ordinary, accept the weapons never arrive at the PE's maintenance department. The ensign, who worked on weapon maintenance became suspicious and reported the matter to Edwards, who in turn told Rebecca.

I alerted the three androids and we met in my home to discuss what measures should be taken.

"Are we sure the weapons are in fact missing?" I asked.

Rebecca nodded. "I checked the vault myself yesterday—they are not there and Edwards has not seen them arrive for maintenance."

Philip interjected. "What do you think Sprack might do? I had thought his plan would be to confront the Committee at one of the general meetings and provide us with some sort of ultimatum. Do you think he is planning an all-out attack?"

"It's difficult to say but I think an all-out attack on the Committee at a meeting might achieve his ends more effectively." I said.

Mike Hunter, the chief security steward put up his hand to speak. "We have the upper hand. They don't think we know anything about their plans. I say let them bring it on."

"We can't assume they don't know anything, Mike. Sprack is not stupid and he must have realized, when his attempts to destroy the androids failed, we knew something was up."

"What do you think he'll do, hon?" asked Carla.

"It's possible he might try to eliminate the major competition in one direct attack but he would need to be confident about the element of surprise. If he attempts something and it fails on the first try, we would easily gain the upper hand with the androids on our side."

Lieutenant Sparkle brought some perspective. *'There has been no further attempt to eliminate the androids—they know we have been upgraded. The records in the PE's maintenance and refurbish logs show this. Of course it doesn't mean they might not try again, since we are the major factor in the colony's protection.'*

Chief Spanner jumped into the conversation. *'If I may add, Mr. Chairman—the Relocation*

Committee is due to meet in three days. To have everyone in the leadership together in one place would be the best time for them to deal a death blow and we should perhaps advertise the fact of requiring all members present, to discuss a very important aspect of business. If a Sprack-sympathizing crowd arrives while the committee is in session Sparkle, Happydoo and I could be in hiding somewhere close by, to intervene.'

I considered Chief Spanner's suggestion. "You're right, Chief. The next meeting would be a good time for them to take control but what if Sprack is present in the meeting? He'll pick up on the absence of the androids and somehow warn his colleagues."

'We could slip out after the meeting has started, Master Beckett. It's normal for androids to stand at the back of the room during the meetings. Perhaps some of the members could stand in a position where Sprack's line of sight would be obstructed. This would allow us to slip out while the meeting is in progress,' said Happydoo.

"I guess it sounds okay. We have no way of knowing their plan. Our young spy says she has not managed to gain access into the top circle, of which there are four people, plus Sprack. She was told, however, to be ready for some future action."

Happydoo said he would inform all the members of the committee to make sure they needed to be present at the meeting and we decid-

ed to set up a plan along the lines of Chief Spanner's suggestion. The three androids would slip out
of the meeting and position themselves in three
different spots between the homes nearest the
meeting hall and we would wait to see if Sprack
made a move. Philip and Rebecca spent some time
talking to Carla after the androids left. I strolled
back to the command pod to think.

A knot formed in my gut when I considered
our current situation. I entertained thoughts of
bringing Sprack in and confronting him with what
we knew, but he would certainly deny the charge
and apart from inflammatory talk against the
model of the colony's government we had no concrete evidence to go on. It would be a mistake to
underestimate the man. Our capabilities of protecting the colony against a rebellion rested in the
power of the three androids. Our security division,
run by Mike Hunter, comprised of three trained
officers, a testimony to the low crime rate. If we
faced a mob of two-hundred and fifty dissenters,
the androids posed our only hope of survival.

The knowledge of the android presence
brought me great comfort. Together they possessed the potential to subdue a much larger
crowd than Sprack's. Due to his military designa-
tion, the lieutenant's original program allowed him
to operate independently of any mode change.
Happydoo and Chief Spanner operated under a
different level of authority and required a change

to make the full scope of the aggressive-mode capability available to them. The codes to change these modes could only be applied by me. The need to have all three androids working together with equal authority, for the present situation, seemed to be the right thing to do. If the shit hit the fan there would be no time for me to reset modes—I decided to set Happydoo and Chief Spanner into aggressive mode with immediate effect.

On arrival at the command pod a surprise awaited me. My dad sat on the rough wooden bench outside the door.

"Hello, Beckett. I know you have lots of things on your mind but I need to talk to you."

"What's up, Dad?"

"I hear through the grapevine we have a problem on our hands. I would like to offer my help."

"You know about the resistance to our governmental model?"

"I know about Sprack. I had several conversations with him over the duration of our voyage and it became evident to me he would end up causing trouble."

My father knew nothing of the planned attempt on lives through the changed protocols of the hibernation process aboard the Andromeda. With the knowledge of Sprack's possible collusion through his association with our ship's refurbishing I decided to share what I believed he was up to.

"Only a few people are aware of the potential threat. We hope to lure Sprack into showing his hand and the possible vehicle for this will be the Establishment Committee meeting in a few days."

"Is there anything I can do," he asked.

I considered the offer. "Yes, in fact there is —would you look after Carla while I attend the committee meeting. I have asked her to stay at home, much to her chagrin. We need to consider her condition."

"Freda and I will come over in the morning before you leave for the meeting. I will bring my own laser."

He hugged me and left. I sat at the console and placed the Cerebral Cortex transmitter on my head for secure communication with the Happy-doo and Chief Spanner. Both answered within seconds.

"Please come to the command pod. I have decided to set you both into aggressive mode."

∞∞

TWENTY-TWO

Anticipation of Insurrection

On the day of the committee meeting I made preparations to leave for the hall. My dad and Freda arrived to stay with a petulant Carla, who wanted to attend but understood the dangers well enough and allowed me to have my way. I ignored her frosty signals and insisted on the safety of our unborn child. After a lengthy discourse in which we both became heated, she finally caved into my request but the air remained a little strained. When I turned to leave she pulled me to her and held on with a tight grip, for several moments, before I broke away with a kiss on her forehead. The tears welled up in her eyes but I could not tell if they represented frustration or fear.

"Mickey will be monitoring the process and I have instructed him to inform you on the omninet if anything sinister happens, but don't worry about—we have the three androids as our backup in case of trouble."

Carla nodded and I left.

Ten minutes later I strolled into the meeting hall, to sit at the head table and await the arrival of our members. The committee consisted of twenty-four people. The total population of the colony, which in all god fortune had suffered little attrition, now stood at over thirty-two hundred people. Many of the second mission's, single personnel, still stayed aboard the Prime Endeavor as more living-units needed to be built. The colony's five building contractors worked four out of five days every week, to provide the accommodation.

The members arrived in groups and took their seats, oblivious to the potential threat of the Sprack rebellion. When Rebecca and Philip arrived, they sat beside me at the head table, while the others faced us.

"I feel bad about Sprack's involvement on the committee. He was unfortunately appointed head of our Political Strategies group by Dr. Abrams, at the beginning of our relocation project," said Rebecca.

"I understand. I remember the forward planning for inclusion of strategists on the Establishment Committee for each arrival group. There was not much you could do about excluding him from committee membership," I said.

Philip made an observation. "I don't see him in the meeting."

"Perhaps a late arrival?" I said.

Rebecca cast a quick glance around the room. "It looks as though everyone else is here."

A feeling of uneasiness crept over me. "We need to start the meeting."

I stood and welcomed everyone. A few of the members stood near the back door in apparent conversation with the three androids who leaned against the back wall, a plan initiated by Sparkle, to create a cover for themselves. With Sprack absented this seemed irrelevant now.

Mickey, by way of video transmission noted all the names of the members present and displayed the agenda on a screen, set up for the purpose. I gave a nod to Lieutenant Sparkle and the three android's slipped quietly through the exit, to disappear into the housing complex. We found it odd that Sprack chose not to be present. It could mean he intended to implement some diabolical plan and might lead the attack. My prior considerations assumed he might rather have chosen to attend, in order to keep an eye on the androids and allow himself to be captured by his sympathizers. But then, again, why would he bother to avert suspicion from himself when the end result would place him in leadership?   It didn't occur to me there might be a different plan. From our spy's observations and conclusions, a direct confrontation between the dissenters and the committee appeared to be on the cards.

The first items on the agenda passed off without any concerns raised and when we reached the fifteen minute recess for refreshments, everyone stood to stretch their legs. I walked to the entrance and peered out at the quadrangle and adjacent houses. While I gazed around the area Happydoo appeared from between two buildings and hastened toward me. I felt the cold clutch of apprehension grip me in its vice and waited for the android to reach the hall entrance.

'Master Beckett, we can't find Mrs. Carla. She isn't at your home where Master Padraig was looking after her.'

I froze. "I left my father and Freda with her —he was armed with a laser and we made no plan for them to go anywhere until I arrived back from the meeting."

'There is no sign of anyone. The front door stood wide open when we arrived—I called out but there was no answer. Lieutenant Sparkle and Chief Spanner are searching all the homes.'

"Something's wrong." I said. "I think they may have been abducted by Sprack and his gang shortly after I left for the meeting hall."

'It must have been before we left the hall to position ourselves amongst the village homes, Master Beckett. When nothing happened for a while I thought I would look in on Mrs. Carla to see that all was in order and found nobody home. I told Sparkle and the Chief before coming straight here.'

"I need to talk to your colleague, the spy. Maybe she might have some idea as to where they would be hiding out. Go and continue the search with the Sparkle and Spanner—I'll grab my CCT from the command pod so I can keep in touch with the three of you."

'I will be happy do that, Master Beckett.' He raced off to join the other two androids.

I returned to the main table where Rebecca and Philip sat waiting for the meeting to resume.

"It looks as though Sprack has outwitted us," I said. I told them of the suspected abduction.

"The androids are searching for them as we speak."

"You must be beside yourself with worry," said Rebecca.

"I'm feeling the pressure but Carla and I have been through some pretty rough situations—she knows how to handle herself. I'm concerned for the safety of our child, though."

"I doubt whether they would harm Carla. If they have taken her I assume they are looking for leverage," said Philip.

I received a CCT transmission from one of the androids. Happydoo's purr sounded inside my brain. 'We have not been able to find them in any of the village homes or businesses, Master Beckett. I have asked Amy, our spy, to meet with you at the hall—she is on the way.'

Amy Watson's knowledge of Sprack's usual meeting places would be a great help but if she couldn't shed any further light on the subject we would be forced to wait for him to contact us.

I decided to close the meeting and cited an emergency situation, which we would inform everyone of later, when more information became available. The members cast questioning glances at me as I left the hall in a hurry and made for our home. I needed to see if any clues might have been left in the wake of the assumed abduction. I arrived to find the front door open as Happydoo originally shared with me. Inside the living room everything appeared to be in its place and the scene showed no evidence of a struggle. This gave me some hope we may be wrong as to the abduction but I spied a light blinking on the holo-platform, which indicated a message on our personal omninet receiver.

I touched the keypad and a hologram of Dr. Sprack appeared on the platform.

"Dr. Conroy. I need to inform you of my intension to contest your leadership of the colony. As you well know, I have made several suggestions as to how things can be improved but these have fallen on deaf ears. You possess an overwhelming advantage with the military might of your androids and I had to find another way to get my message through to you. You will notice your wife, father and his spouse are no longer where you left them this morning. I have them in

a safe place and they will not be harmed providing you listen to reason. I will be contacting you shortly with a few of our demands.

Sprack out."

I stared at the platform for several moments after the hologram dissipated into a fuzzy cloud and disappeared. My gut churned inside, concerned for the safety of my loved ones—the fact of being outsmarted also hit hard. I should have anticipated this sort of action from Sprack. A knock on the door revealed an anxious Amy Watson, our spy.

"Dr. Conroy? I'm sorry to disturb you but Happydoo said you wanted to talk to me? I went straight to the meeting hall but President Commander Cruse said you would be here."

"Come in, Amy and sit down for a moment. First of all—thank you for helping us with information regarding the problem we are facing with Sprack and his rebels."

"It's my pleasure and civic duty, Sir. How can I further help you?"

"Do you know of any possible place Dr. Sprack and his followers might hold hostages?"

She hesitated and then answered. "I doubt whether they would use any place in the village. We always met at the Dungeon Cafteen bar and out on the farm, but these places are too obvious.

May I suggest you solicit the help of the forest dwellers."

She hit the nail on the head. The forest dwellers knew the movement of all things within our designated areas of hunting, fishing and general recreation which involved the many hiking trails. Charley and Lucy would know the whereabouts of Sprack, or any of his people, if they ventured beyond the village perimeter.

"Thanks for your input, Amy. I'll follow up on your suggestion right away."

"Let me know if there's anything else I can do, Mr. Chairman," she said. We shook hands and she left.

The CCT signal sent to Lieutenant Sparkle, made contact with the android's processor within milliseconds.

"Make immediate contact with Charley and Lucy. Find out if they know of any movement of humans within the forest, Abrams Lake, or the mountain caves."

'We are on our way to Charley's domain, Sir. I will let you know,' answered Sparkle.

With nothing further to be achieved at home I walked back to the command pod. Another avenue for me to follow up on came to mind—our camera's situated on the two mountain tops which hid the antimatter canons. These commanded a view of the entire territory around the mountains and also skyward. Mickey responded to my request and set both cameras on a continuous sweep of the terrain. For at least an hour, I watched every detail of the surrounding areas like a hawk in the hope of spotting something suspicious, but to no avail.

A CCT signal resounded in my brain with a sudden internal sensation, which caused me a split-second of mental discomfort.

∞∞

TWENTY-THREE

Sprack's Demands

Lieutenant Sparkle's deep tone tickled my faculties. *'Charley and Lucy report they have seen a group of people moving through the forest toward a certain area at the base of the tallest mountain, Mr. Chairman. Charley nearly had a heart attack when we told him what was happening. He says at least ten unidentified people are involved.'*

"Can Charley tell us exactly where these people have gone?"

'Unfortunately not, Mr. Chairman—only that they were headed in the general direction of the tallest mountain.'

"Where are you and the other two droids at the moment, Lieutenant?"

'We're at the farm, Sir. I'll take Chief Spanner with me and search the base of the mountain and its cave system. I suggest Happydoo return to the village in case another part of the group try an attack.'

"Good thinking, Sparkle. Let me know if you find anything."

My eye reverted back to the holographic display of the terrain. "Mickey—concentrate both cameras on the base of the largest mountain. Let's see if anything comes up. I suspect the enemy might be using a cave system as a hiding place for the hostages."

'As you request, Mr. Chairman.'

The cameras both focused in on the target area and I searched the cliff faces and crags for any signs but nothing out of the ordinary came to light.

"Is there anything further on my home omninet system, Mickey?"

'Two messages, Mr. Chairman. I see you have already listened to one of them.'

"I have listened to the one left by Sprack, regarding the abduction of my family. Let me hear the second one."

Sprack's voice once again boomed forth from the holo-platform. His face appeared impassive.

"Greetings, Dr. Conroy.

I promised you a list of the things our group feels is necessary, to make the colony a more open and democratic society. If you acquiesce to these principles we'll meet and hold a discussion. I must inform you we are over two-hundred and fifty people strong. Many of us are armed and ready to fight for our rights. I will not hesitate to harm your family if you resist. Here are our demands:

One: The three androids will be decommissioned before any other negotiation takes place.

Two: You and the Committee will open yourselves to a democratic process—a vote, if you like. The colony's qualified voting members will choose a government, subject to certain criteria of a constitution which we will jointly draw up.

Three: You will personally submit yourself to a legal process by a judiciary, chosen by the voters, to determine your negligence in the loss of life aboard the Andromeda during the tenure of your mission project. Principally, you will need to answer for the death of the Andromeda's Executive Officer, Gary Pearson.

Four: A Police force will be established to protect the new arrangements. Your answer is required by mid-day tomorrow on this frequency. Your Master Computer will be able to pinpoint the coordinates from where this signal was sent but it won't help you to find us.

Sprack out."

"You heard the message, Mickey—why will pinpointing the co-ords for this signal not help us to locate these bastards?"

'Because when they broadcasted the signal they were on the move—by the time we arrive at *the general area of transmission they will be long gone, Mr. Chairman.'*

"That Sprack shithouse is getting under my skin. I swear if I get my hands on his scrawny throat he'll be a gonner."

'You will want to call a meeting of those on the Committee you can trust, Boss. We don't know how many of the members share Sprack's sentiments.'

"Right now, the only people I trust are Philip and Rebecca Cruse—and the three androids, of course. Call them to the command pod immediately."

'Aye, aye, Boss.'

"Also launch one of the weather drones and use the heat-signature application—let's see if we can find any evidence of life in the system of caves."

To say I bordered on panic would have been an understatement. Fear of harm to my family spilled over into my usual calm, rational response to a crisis. We appeared to be at a huge disadvantage, despite the android factor. I sat at the console with my head in my hands and contemplated the worst scenario for an outcome. I could not risk the lives of my family for a concept of government rule. A democratic model would work until power and greed got in the way. It allowed ideologies to flourish and the balance of power always ended up in the hands of the rich.

After the great war of 2135, harmful ideologies were eradicated and a new dynamic of controlled advancement in all forms of human endeavor, arose. The inclusion of a Master Computer, to police the New World Earth and run the aspirations of human beings in conjunction with The Administration, worked well for everyone. Although I hated The Administration for what they did to my family life, the system kept humans in a state of low competition but high fulfilment.

I brooded for some time until a knock on the pod entrance by Philip, jerked me back to reality.

He looked tired. "We came as soon as Mickey called. What's happened, Beckett?"

I shared the news of Sprack's demands with them and repeated the news to Happydoo on his arrival.

"What do you intend to do, Beckett?" asked Rebecca.

"We need to discuss the situation together and come up with a plan we all agree on—it's my family's lives on the line and changes in our government system, will affect everyone."

"Are you thinking of conceding to Sprack's demands?" asked Philip.

"Not at this point."

Lieutenant Sparkle and Chief Spanner made their appearance and waited for us to acknowledge their presence.

"Find anything so far, Lieutenant?"

'No, Mr. Chairman. We checked out a few of the caves used by the colony for a hiding place when the alien's invaded, but there was no sign of Dr. Sprack or his people.'

"There are a lot of caves in the base of that mountain—I have asked Mickey to launch a weather drone and scan the area for heat signatures."

'It will not be conclusive, Mr. Chairman. There are quite a few different creatures living in the caves.' said Chief Spanner.

"I'm aware of that, Chief but we need to explore every avenue."

Rebecca ran a wiry hand through her white hair. "The safety of your family is of the utmost importance. What if we agreed to talk about changes in the political system and see if a compromise can be reached?"

"I am prepared to consider it as a last resort. Sprack has asked for the decommissioning of the androids and we can't allow that. He may also want to use the Prime Endeavor as a Base—I suspect it would be useful to him and his agenda to control the colony."

Happydoo raised a bionic hand. 'I have a suggestion, Master Beckett. When you contact Dr. Sprack tomorrow tell him you will acquiesce to all the demands and gain some time for us to find their position. Charley has told me, he and the forest dwellers are well acquainted with the cave systems. If the drone picks up a large heat signature the dwellers might know of an alternate route for a rescue.'

"But he wants an immediate decommission of the three of you."

'It depends on how much expertise he has on the decommission process,' said Sparkle.

Happydoo continued. 'It is as the Lieutenant says, Master Beckett. Only someone involved in the latest programs running the D2000 processors, will know there is a function available to decommission the main program on a timer. It allows for the main power system to be removed completely, but leaves a backup function.'

Lieutenant Sparkle concluded. 'When the main power source is removed, the limited auxiliary power system for running sensors and secondary-systems will keep the android in a suspended animated form.'

"You are saying we can decommission you without completely removing your abilities to function?" I asked.

Chief Spanner took his turn. 'We would be able to function in a very limited way after the timer reactivates us back to service mode and some movement capability will remain. From there, if we are able to gain access to a main power source again, we will have normal access to our abilities.'

"So, if we decommission you and provide additional power sources for you to get your hands on, you will be back to full operation again?"

'That is correct, Mr. Chairman,' said Sparkle.

Philip jumped in. "It's risky but worth a try. At least we can gain some time for the androids to get back into contention."

Mickey broke the conversation with a sudden comment.

'Mr. Chairman. I am detecting a sudden presence at the fringe of the solar system. I believe we might have company.'

∞∞

TWENTY-FOUR

Alien Revenge

The words came with the force of a hurricane. The news could not have come at a more inopportune time and my worst fears sprung up like ocean spray in a wind storm. The sudden silence in the command pod deafened us as we stared incomprehensibly at each other. For several moments no one spoke. The reality of the possibilities raged against my common sense and although we expected the arrival of the next Earth mission sometime in the near future the alternative, a Crustan invasion, would be unthinkable.

I found my voice. "What are we going to do now?"

Rebecca looked at me with alarm. "Who do you think it might be? It's too early for the third Earth mission."

"Only one possibility, I'm afraid—the return of a Crustan force—the aliens who attacked us previously. If it is them they will come with much greater numbers this time."

Philip squinted at the hologram Mickey set up for our benefit. It showed the outer reaches of the Peg 51 solar system, with five planets in an almost straight line and further out an asteroid belt similar to the one between Mars and Jupiter.

"What do you mean by much greater numbers?"

"The last time they were here, a short time before your arrival there were seven warships and we destroyed six with our antimatter canon. We had the element of surprise and caught them off-guard. The one that escaped will have warned them of the status of our weaponry and this time they will be prepared."

I held up my hand to silence Rebecca's next question and addressed Mickey. "How far out are they? How long do we have, before whoever it is, arrives?"

'We have eight days at the present velocity of approach, Mr. Chairman.'

"We have eight days to resolve the Sprack crises. Keep me informed of any changes in the alien's velocity and the identity of the force as soon as you are able."

'I should know the identity within fifty hours, Boss.'

"I suggest we put it out of our minds for the moment and concentrate on a game plan to deal with the rebellion. I will send Sprack a message, first light tomorrow, to talk about his demands. We'll play for time and hope the drone or the forest dwellers can come up with a location."

Philip countered my suggestion. "Perhaps we should inform Sprack of a possible alien invasion and get him to hold off on the decommissioning of the droids."

I did not think this to be a good idea. "He'll think we're playing for time. It will be slightly more than another two days, before we can even identify the force and I'm afraid Sprack might harm my family."

"Perhaps it's better we put the aliens out of our minds for the moment and see what we can negotiate with Sprack," said Rebecca.

The light behind Lieutenant Sparkle's eyes oscillated vociferously. 'What about the decommissioning, Mr. Chairman?'

I hesitated. The possible arrival of an alien force on our doorstep and the thought of a confrontation without the androids frightened the shit out of me. A decision needed to be made.

"We have little option but to go for it, Lieutenant and hope we can pull off your recommission before the alien force arrives."

I will go to the Prime Endeavor and speak to Chief Edwards. Only he can arrange for three separate power packs to be stored in a place of our choosing, Mr. Chairman,' said Sparkle.

Happydoo interjected. 'Are we sure Chief Edwards is on our side, Master Beckett?'

I looked at Philip and Rebecca for confirmation. The both affirmed Chief Edward's loyalty.

"I will discuss the decommissioning with Sprack, to see how he wants to handle it. I suspect he would like to see the process with his own eyes and take over the main power packs, to ensure your immobility.

"What if we can't find where your family is been kept?" questioned Rebecca.

"It's a river I don't want to cross at the moment. We will have to wait and see."

Our meeting ended in somber silence. No more could be said and we all went our different ways, Rebecca and Philip to the PE and the androids to the charge station hut, to park themselves for the night. I walked back to our home and thought of Carla and our unborn child. The churning in my gut made me want to weep. Would I ever become a parent? Would I ever see my wife alive again and what if the Crustans attacked us before the rebellion could be resolved. With all these questions swirling around in my mind, I entered our home to a quietness which emphasized the desolation of the moment and replayed Sprack's demands on the holo-platform. It took all my willpower to resist the temptation to grab the three-D image by the throat and throttle the hologram into oblivion.

The night passed at a snail's pace due to much anxious deliberation. In the morning I dressed and ordered some cafteen from the food and beverage replicator, in the kitchen. After activation of the holo-platform the coordinates given by Sprack brought the hateful image before me and I steeled myself to negotiate. Sprack appeared without any delay, his face a picture of calm. I repulsed the temptation to swear and waited for him to begin the conversation.

"Greetings, Dr. Conroy." I remained silent and kept my emotions in check. He continued.

"I know you will be angry about what has taken place but we are of two different frames of mind so I will spare you casual conversation and get to the point.

"Please do, Sprack," I said. The tone of my voice carried the malevolence I felt toward the man. His facial features remained unchanged.

"Have you considered our demands?"

I nodded and said nothing.

"And you are prepared to acquiesce to all of them?"

I hesitated. "What choice do I have, Sprack—you are holding my family hostage, which I must remind you, is a heinous and cowardly act."

"As I said, Dr. Conroy, you will be angry and I don't blame you, however, we have something to accomplish and as much as I hate violence I consider the ends to justify the means. Let's talk about the demands."

I waited for him to continue. *"The first and most important is the decommissioning of the androids. There is really no use for them in society and if we are to preserve the human element in the long run, this is a necessity."*

"I have found the androids to be most useful so I have a different perspective," I said.

"I would like to accomplish this as a sign of your compliance. The power packs are to be removed from their processors in my presence. I don't care what you do with the robots after that."

I hesitated—it sounded as though Sprack was not aware of the timer arrangement in the D2000.

"Where do you want to do this? All I want is for you to release the hostages. I am prepared to acquiesce to all the rest of your demands, under duress of course, in order to have my family released."

Sprack smiled. *"I knew you would see reason, Dr. Conroy. Tomorrow we'll meet in the village quadrangle, where you will remove the power packs and hand them over to me. I also want to make an arrangement to speak with your Establishment Committee. They will be disbanded in lieu of an electoral college."*

"Whatever—when will you release my family?"

"When I am satisfied things are on the right track. I am sure you will try to double cross me at some point during this negotiation."

"This is not a negotiation. It's a railroading."

"It doesn't matter what name you give it, Dr. Conroy—the end result will be a better system for everyone."

"So it will." I meant something quite different to his frame of reference.

"I will be in the quadrangle at noon, tomorrow. Make sure everything is as it should be and your loved ones will be safe. I have no desire to harm them."

"You had better not—I'll be there."

*

At noon on the following day we all assembled in the quadrangle. I put out a message to the Committee and twenty-one people gathered, inclusive of myself and the three androids. Sprack arrived with two of his henchmen, smug in the fact they held all the aces. The process of decommissioning took on a ceremonial atmosphere. My heart felt heavy at the loss of my friends, even though I knew it would only be temporary—or so I hoped.

Mike Hunter, our chief security supervisor removed the power packs from each android's cranium and it unnerved me to see them go limp with a sudden collapse of limbs. Some of Mike's helpers moved the now impotent AI's, to their charging hut and left them, face-down, on the ground. I felt like a murderer. Chief Edwards of the PE's maintenance promised he would have the new power-packs available within hours of the decommissioning and everyone trooped into the hall to be seated for Sprack's talk. After a few moments he traipsed in and stood behind the head table to face his audience. I could see him visibly bask in the presence of all the inquisitive stares. Not one else, to my knowledge, knew about Sprack's rebellion or his demands and they all relaxed to listen.

"My dear fellow colonists. As you know, I have had a fundamental difference of opinion with the model of government you have all suffered under since your arrival on Hera-soter. I realize for some of you the decommissioning of the androids might have come as a surprise but it was an essential first step, in the rectification of the many mistakes made by your chairman, Dr. Conroy."

Several of the members glanced over at me to see what my reaction to his inflammatory statement would be. I did not react and maintained a stony silence.

He continued his victory speech. "As from today things will change for the better. The Establishment Committee will be disbanded as the governing body and an electoral college will be instituted in its place. The college will oversee a democratic process for a better system of government."

He turned and smiled at me. "Dr. Conroy—now for your greatest surprise yet. The people whom you thought supported you have never been supporters at all. The entire leadership of the PE is in fact, on my side."

My mouth fell open and hope abandoned me in an instant as I turned to stare at Philip and Rebecca. They sat impassively looking at Sprack—neither would look me in the eye. I couldn't believe it. All this time they had been leading me on. Sprack knew every detail of our plan. This meant Edwards would not come up with the battery packs and the androids would not be coming to my aid. My heart almost failed and my breathing started to labor as I looked around like a rat on a ship, about to sink. I had been a fool from the beginning and the incrimination of it all over-whelmed me.

"Dr. Conroy, you will be taken and placed in the PE's brig until we're ready to hear your case. The Electoral College will elect Hera-soter's first legal cabinet and appoint a judicial enquiry into your leadership."

"I stammered and stuttered out a few curse words as I stood to my feet, intent on making a bolt for the exit.

Sprack's cold eyes belied the smile on his lips. "Your leadership of the first Mission Project was not accepted by all those in The Administra-tion and had it not been for Dr. Abrams, your ap-plication would have been rejected."

He turned to two men sitting, one on each side of me. "Take him to the PE's brig and lock him up."

The men grabbed my arms and roughly dragged me toward the exit. I could see the shocked look of many of the council members, in obvious shock. One or two stood to their feet to object, but Sprack's hostile voice rose above the sounds of my garbled threats.

"If anyone is in disagreement with this ruling please make your objections known after the meeting."

The members sat down again in confusion while Sprack's guards took me out of the building and threw me to the ground. They started to kick me and I tried to protect my vulnerable parts but the two intended to give me a beating. Before long I blacked out.

∞∞

TWENTY-FIVE

In The Brig

The PE's brig looked similar to the Andromeda's. Carla and I spent some time in our ship's cell when my executive officer, Gary Pearson, tried to initiate a take-over, before our arrival on Hera-soter. My body hurt all over. When I tried to roll over onto my stomach, several bruised ribs complained bitterly at the attempt. I slumped onto my back to ease the pain and contemplated my predicament. Without the help of the androids my case for an escape appeared hopeless. Why had I not suspected Rebecca and Philip? They had played their parts well but I couldn't figure out why they would fall prey to the political sentiments of a person like Sprack. Something strange appeared to be afoot but my situation displayed the cold, hard facts—my incarceration as ludicrous as it seemed, posed a present reality, a condition I could do nothing about.

I considered the plight of my family. What would Sprack do with them? I didn't think he would harm Carla, other than bring her up on similar charges. It would not be advantages for him to appear as a dictator while at the same time he attempted to institute a democratic process of government. I failed to see why he would want to champion a failed political system—one that had led to several world wars and the Great War of 2135. Since that time, years of fine genetic tuning had provided delegates, destined from infants, to be leaders. Technology programs, written for participating android members, focused on excellent leadership and service to humans as a whole. Sprack's argument, which they claimed to be one of a moral nature still existed among a few dissidents—those who remained stuck in the political grooves of previous centuries.

The problem of a pending Crustan attack also plagued me. Philip and Rebecca would have informed Sprack about this but no one knew the strength of the Crustans better than we did. Not that we could prevent the attack if it came, but we could at least prepare a better defense than any of the recent PE arrivals. I dragged myself through the pain onto a bunk, which protruded from one wall of the cell and lay down to think.

*

I'm not sure of the time or the day when Sprack came to see me. The brig, in the depth of the starship's belly gave no indication of time's passage, other than the meals I received.

"Greetings, Dr. Conroy. I see you are in good shape."

I stared at him with hostile intent and remained seated on my bunk.

"I've come to prepare you for your trial. It will take place the day after tomorrow but first I have a few questions."

I continued to stare at him without saying anything.

"I believe we are about to be invaded by an alien force which will apparently be here in a few days. I know you experienced a few altercations with this group before and somehow you survived. It may seem audacious of me to ask, but since you already have an experience with these creatures, would you be willing on behalf of the colony's safety, to share how you overcame them."

I considered his request. "No, I don't think I would be willing to share anything with you, Sprack. You take my wife and father hostage and trump up some silly charge against me regarding my leadership, then expect me to cooperate with you—you can go fuck yourself."

Sprack's expression remained calm. "I understand your frustration, Conroy but the entire Colony is at stake here unless we can prepare a good defense. I will see to it, your father and wife are freed of any charges, if you will consider to trade with me."

I stood to my feet. "You are wrong about Gary Pearson, Sprack. He committed the crime of mutiny which is a death sentence in any legal system. His plan to seize the Andromeda failed, after an attempt to have my wife and I murdered."

"We will go into all that at your trial, Conroy. I am making an offer with regard to your family."

My mind raced to size up the reality of our situation. "Why should I trust you, Sprack?"

"You have no option but to trust me—right now I have all the aces up my sleeve. I have great respect for your father and the work he has achieved—I feel he will still be useful to the colony. Your wife is pregnant, I understand. You owe it to your unborn child to do what you can for the protection of the people."

I could not deny the veracity of Sprack's statements. "Okay, you have a point. I will advise you on the threat the colony is facing but let's be clear—I'm doing it for the people and not for you."

He gave me a thin smile. His cold, dark eyes exuded victory. "Good, Dr. Conroy. I'm glad you are finally seeing the truth of the matter. Now, what can you share regarding this alien threat.

A short summary of the first attacks on the Andromeda ensued as I explained the use of the antimatter canon's first use in space warfare. I did not explain how we came to be in possession of the technology. I told him about the two anti-matter canons perched in strategic places on the two mountains close to the village.

"The Crustans will have realized we possess such a weapon and are bound to have some sort of answer for it." I said. "In conclusion our only hope, if they use a ground force, will be the three androids you have so misguidedly decommissioned."

He stood quietly and stared at me in assessment of the picture my words painted.

"So, the antimatter canon worked well when it was used?"

"It only worked because we had the element of surprise. As I have said, we no longer possess that element. The Crustans are an extremely advanced species and if they come in overwhelming numbers, our two canons will not cope."

For the first time Sprack seemed concerned about the colony's prospects of survival and he appeared conflicted.

"We will have to see what happens then. I doubt if I could agree to the use of the androids should they invade us with a ground force."

To reinforce some reality I moved forward and stared into his eyes. Only the transparent force-field separated us from each other.

"You will have little choice, Sprack. The Crustans have nukes and lasers, equal to our own. If you're thinking of using the PE, forget it—they'll blast it out of the sky before you get out of the atmosphere."

"But we will have some protection from the force field installed above the village?"

"You will have limited protection for a time but if you are not going to use the androids I suggest you hide in the caves and hope the enemy can't find you."

He looked uncertain and I felt a brief sensation of smugness which disappeared before my ego could assimilate it. The truth of the matter negated any shallow victory for my self-esteem.

"I thank you for sharing these details with me. I will stick to my offer and allow your family to go free once your trial is over. We are setting up a court in the meeting hall for your benefit. This afternoon an appointed legal counselor will visit with you and you can prepare your case but don't get your hopes up—we have overwhelming evidence of your guilt."

He walked away without another word—I felt confused and perplexed.

Later in the afternoon a woman, by the name of Loretta Baines, paid me a visit. One of the PE group, she introduced herself as my appointed lawyer. A tough looking guard raised a hand laser to point at my chest as he deactivated the force-field to give her access to the cell. Loretta sat on the end of the bunk and placed a metal briefcase on the floor. Her soft spoken voice brought an air of quiet deliberation into the brig and had it not been for the circumstances I would have enjoyed the encounter. We discussed the details of the charge levelled against me and she spoke a few short sentences into a CCT transmitter which I assumed transferred to a computer somewhere on the ship. I related the entire story of Gary Pearson's mutiny which followed the attempt by someone involved in the Andromeda's refurbishing, to murder Carla and I. Loretta asked a few questions and I got the distinct notion she possessed empathy for my situation. After an upward glance at the cell's camera, she gave me a look of enquiry and I knew there was more to her presence than my legal concerns.

"I will see you in court the day after tomorrow. I want you to know I will do my best with the information you have given me. I am also going to speak to your wife for corroboration of the facts you have supplied. Is there any other person whom I could speak to?"

"My android valet has recorded all the facts. If by any chance you can get a power pack to activate its processor, you will find everything you need," I said.

She looked nervously up at the camera gain. "I will have to get permission from Dr. Sprack for that but I'll certainly do my best."

"Please tell my wife—her name is Carla—I love her very much and not to give up hope," I asked.

She nodded and stuck out her hand. To my surprise she held onto my fingers, gave them a squeeze and whispered, "You have friends, Beckett."

After shaking hands Loretta turned and called for the guard. Her nervous glances at the camera and the way she looked at me, the squeeze of my fingers—all these nuances conveyed a message of some sort.

Dare I hope her to be sympathetic enough to help me?

∞∞

TWENTY-SIX

The Trial

The day of the trial arrived. Two guards came, shackled my hands and escorted me back to the village. The villagers stood in a line and watched as the guards walked me up the hall steps and into the building. Loretta, seated at a table on one side of the hall, stood to greet me and we sat down to await the trial.

"Carla sends her love," said the lawyer.

I smiled and asked, "How is she?"

"She is just fine. Both her and the baby are doing well."

I sat back in my seat and closed my eyes. I wanted so badly to be with Carla. It felt as though my heart would break.

The courtroom, filled up with people. Most belonged to the Prime Endeavor's mission but I could see several faces I recognized from the original journey. Along the walls three men with lasers, stood with watchful eyes on the crowd, ready for any signs of trouble. This assured me Sprack did not have a run-away vote of confidence. This court hearing may seem an appropriate measure to take but it could backfire on him. If it did not go his way I'm sure brute force would be the final consideration and I would still find myself on death-row.

A man I did not recognize stood to quieten everyone down, while Sprack and two of his cronies entered the building, to take seats at the head table. I scanned the crowd. Philip and Rebecca sat in the middle of the third row, with downcast looks and sad eyes. They would not look at me. I wondered what sort of gun Sprack held to their heads in order to have gained such cooperation. They came across as upright, good people who cared for those under their command. The turn-about of allegiance troubled me—I wanted to hate them but I couldn't. The hall held about two hundred and fifty people with the majority of the colony members outside, hoping to get some news of the trial.

The man I did not recognize appeared to be the counsel for the prosecution. He brought the meeting to order and read out the charge.

"The prisoner, Dr. Beckett Conroy, is charged with the murder of his executive officer, Lieutenant Commander Gary Pearson and over seven hundred members of the Andromeda's compliment. The prosecution will prove willful negligence on behalf of Dr. Conroy, while in leadership of the first relocation project mission and the handling of a battle against alien forces, before the establishment of the Hera-sotern Colony. Details of the logs obtained from the Andromeda's Master Computer will show that Dr. Conroy deliberately provoked the alien force by firing on them first."

Loretta reached over and squeezed my hand before she stood to rebut the prosecutions charges.

"I would like to place on record that the records of the Andromeda's Master Control Computer give the appearance of having been altered in a way to support the prosecution's case."

I glanced up at the head table where Sprack sat beside a man and a woman whom I took to be the selected judges for the trial. I did not know if Sprack had a legal background but I guessed him to be setting up the groundwork in order to oil his way into the presidency of their first democratically elected government. The trial wore on with Loretta producing a conflicting record from Happydoo's processor. Sprack must have given her permission to pull this testimony from the android. The battle of submissions and rebuttals continued for two hours but in the end the weight of falsified evidence against me swung the pendulum in favor of the prosecution and hope of a fair result ended with Sprack banging a homemade gavel on a piece of wood. "We have heard enough evidence to bring about a fair decision and the prisoner is permitted to speak."

Loretta nudged me. I stood with a slow deliberation and faced the courtroom crowd.

"I have served as chairman of the Establishment Committee, for several years, in accordance with the mandate provided me by Dr. Abrams of the Relocation project. Those of you who spaced in the Andromeda with me know I am man of integrity. I deeply regret the loss of life during my command but these were not circumstance under my control. And for my XO—he was a lying son-of-a bitch, who brought about a mutiny on our ship and tried to take over command of the vessel. This court hearing is a farce and set up to dispose of me so that Dr. Sprack can fulfil his own devious ambition."

I sat down. You could have heard a pin drop. No one spoke as one of the judges stood to address the crowd.

"The judicial panel will now deliver its findings. We find the prisoner Dr. Conroy, guilty of murder in the first degree. According to paragraph LGL2401 of the Space Command Penal Code—as President Commander of the Andromeda, he did not fulfill his duties in an honorable way and thereby caused the death of seven-hundred and twelve of the ship's compliment."

I looked at her in astonishment. This could not be happening. I turned to Loretta who closed her eyes in frustration at the obvious falsity of the case against me. I wanted to confer with her but Sprack stood, to make a statement.

"It has been decided by my esteemed colleagues and I, that sentence will be passed right away, a caveat to the standard procedure of the Penal Code, which would normally allow for a space of several days before sentencing takes place. The prisoner is hereby sentenced to death by an appointed laser-squad."

Loretta jumped up from the table and protested in a loud voice but two of the guards restrained her. She continued to struggle and scream her indignation at the suddenness of the sentence.

"This is a legal catastrophe," she shouted. The people erupted into an uproar of contention but one of the guards shot a laser bolt into the floor to bring order. Two guards led me through the midst of the people and out onto the landing where I faced the crowd, outside. When news of the sentence reached their ears a murmur arose which developed into shouts of disagreement and for a moment I hoped there might be a riot.

A group of thirty guards, armed with weapons, stepped up to encircle me as they moved into the quadrangle. The guards moved the people away to the perimeter and I stood, shackled by the wrists and waited for my sentence to be carried out. The tallest of the men cautioned his comrades to back up and give him space as he raised the rifle-laser and pointed it at my chest. The crowd booed and shouted obscenities. A few of the men, some whom I recognized as Andromeda staff members railed at him but the others fired a few laser charges of discouragement. Bits of dirt and red grass, mingled with smoke, plumed into the air and the crowd retreated.

My final thoughts focused on Carla and my unborn child. They say, at the moment before death, your life parades before your eyes but all I could think of was my family. I felt no fear, only sadness. A final consolation came in the form of a philosophical consideration—I had never been a religious person but this last thought centered on my unborn child. Whatever came after death, it could only be a better life than the one we knew—I would be reunited with my loved ones in another form.

I heard the click of the laser's power regulator. With a final glance around at the many faces in the crowd I raised my eyes to the sky. High up, on the edge of the atmosphere, I saw a flash of light as the Andromeda caught the rays of Peg 51—I waited for death to take me away.

∞∞

TWENTY-SEVEN

A Close Call

Interminable seconds passed as I waited for the blast to end my life. I closed my eyes in the hope of diminished pain and heard a strange noise like a puff of smoke, accompanied by sizzling flesh. Strange—I felt no pain at all. I opened my eyes to see a mysterious sight. The tall guard, who moments before held the laser pointed straight at me, lay in a crumpled mass of burning flesh. People in the crowd screamed in fright as a figure marched into the quad amongst them. My brain would not compute. I appeared to be dreaming, or maybe I was already dead and this illusion remained as a figment of an afterlife.

My knees gave way beneath me and my body, immobilized by shock, toppled to the ground. The people shouted with one accord, accompanied by explosions of laser strikes which came from a sound I instinctively recognized. I remembered the sound the twin beams had made when Lieutenant Sparkle struck down the Crustans as they attacked us.

A hard pair of hands grabbed my arms and turned me over onto my back. *'Master Beckett. Are you okay?'*

I opened my eyes again and stared into Happydoo's two blue, oscillating orbs.

"You have a habit of turning up at the oddest times," I murmured.

The broad grin twisted the synthetic skin to the limit as the android propped me up in its arms. *'As you know, Master Beckett—I am always happy to do that.'*

"What happened—how in heaven's name did you get recommissioned?"

'It's a long story, Master Beckett. I must see that order is restored before we can sit down and have a chat.'

I looked past the android to see Chief Spanner, staring the guards down, all of whom had dropped their weapons in fear of being roasted alive. On the steps of the hall stood Lieutenant Sparkle with a man in his clutches—Sprack. Several of the guards, who tried to retaliate, lay smoldering on the grass near the building. Sprack broke free from the android's grip and charged down the steps in an attempt to escape. The Lieutenant cut him down with one charge and he fell to the ground, to lie inert, with a plume of smoke over his head.

"I think your friends have already restored order. It looks like the end of Dr. Sprack's ambitions," I said.

*

An hour later I sat in the command pod with Happydoo, Loretta Baines, Mike Hunter and a few others while Chief Spanner and a group of people cleared up the carnage at the hall. Lieutenant Sparkle and a jubilant Charley had left to rescue my family from one of the cave systems on directions from one of Sprack's guards. The Lieutenant would take care of any resistance—two of Sprack's guards still remained, guarding the hostages.

I turned to Happydoo. "Please tell me how this all went down. How did you do it?"

The android raised an open hand to Loretta and cocked his head in typical AI fashion. *'Miss Loretta?'*

Loretta Baines smiled sheepishly. "I am not who I pretended to be. The story started many years ago during the refurbishing of your vessel, the Andromeda. We suspected something sinister was afoot which included   Dr. Sprack's involvement—nothing could be proved at the time but as a precaution the New World Earth Intelligence Agency placed me in the field to watch certain people—Sprack being one of them."

I must have looked confused. "I thought you were a lawyer?"

"I studied basic law before I joined the EIA and became an operative."

"You must have known my wife, Carla?"

"Actually, no—she was before my time. To get back to our story, Dr. Sprack made several comments which placed a suspicion on some of the Prime Endeavor's compliment. These comments led the EIA to believe he was planning a take-over of the colony on Hera-soter so, I was placed on the mission under the guise of a lawyer."

I digested the information. "Did you know Philip and Rebecca Cruse were on Sprack's team?"

Loretta pursed her lips for a moment. "Rebecca and Philip were never on Sprack's team to begin with. These are two good people who got caught up in an unfortunate circumstance which Sprack manipulated—he blackmailed them."

I experienced a twinge of relief but still did not feel entirely convinced. "They certainly played their parts well. I was convinced they had taken me for a ride."

"I will let Rebecca tell you their story herself. Both she and Philip feel terrible about what they had to do but she believed there to be no choice."

"Did you re-activate the androids, somehow?" I asked.

"Chief Edwards, of the Prime Endeavor's maintenance, was not on Sprack's team—although Sprack thought he could trust Edwards. The Chief is also a member of the EIA and we were working together on Sprack's case."

I put two and two together. "So, Philip and Rebecca never told Sprack about the timer-delay restart, or the plan to recommission the droids?"

"No—Sprack never knew anything about it. I wanted to share more with you when we met in the cell but because of the guard's presence and the sensitivity of the camera I decided to trust my instincts about you."

"Your instincts?" I asked.

"Your mission members have told me a lot about you and Carla. I knew you would remain calm and not give up."

I grinned. "You and the droids certainly left things right to the last minute."

"It took time to arrange the new power pack systems. We also had to deal with the guard who had been commissioned by Sprack to destroy the androids. Edwards and I only managed to save them in the nick of time. Then, we had to reprogram their military functions and reboot their processors."

I heard a sound at the pod entrance and Lieutenant Sparkle stepped through the doorway. I jumped up and rushed past him to feast my eyes on the most heartwarming spectacle of my life—

Carla stood there with a huge grin on her face. We collapsed into one another's arms and for several moments we gave vent to our emotions. Tears flowed as I held the love of my life and swore never to allow her out of my sight again. My dad and Freda gathered around us and we all enjoyed a group hug.

*

Later, in the evening, the entire colony met in the quadrangle for a special meeting. I needed to clear the air and let everyone know we would continue in the normal way.

I looked at the solemn faces and felt like a father who needed to comfort his children.

"The rebellion is over. I want nothing more than for everything to revert back to normal. The Establishment Committee will resume its over-sight of the colony and the perpetrators will be dealt with in an appropriate way, but we are not out of the woods yet. I will have an announcement to make within a few days. I ask those of you who involved with Dr. Sprack, please come clean and take a vow of commitment to the colony's leader-ship. A panel, under the leadership of my wife, Carla Conroy and Loretta Baines will convene to-morrow morning, in the meeting hall. You will talk to them about your involvement and a decision will be made as to what the outcome should be."

Philip and Rebecca Cruse came to see me privately to share their story. They were never an intricate part of the rebellion—and would be happy to serve some sort of community time to make up for the trauma their involvement foisted on the colony. Rebecca broke down in tears and explained how Sprack had planted a nuclear device with its own security system, on the PE. If the couple did not toe the line, the explosive would be detonated remotely to destroy all on aboard. Sprack had at first required their allegiance to his penchant for android destruction, before his real intentions of replacing the Establishment Committee were revealed.

When the latter took on its more ominous form of a rebellion they realized they were trapped and wanted to ask my for help. Sprack warned them if they made any move to inform us he would kill Carla and our unborn child.

"It's good to get this whole mess out of the way," I said. Carla and I forgave our friends and hugged them.

Carla brought us all back to the present. "We still have a crisis ahead of us. We have unwelcomed visitors, who will be in range for identification within a day. Mickey will let us know at the earliest opportunity."

*

Two days later Mickey gave me the bad news. *'A huge force of Crustan Warships are within fifty billion kilometers of the planet, Mr. Chairman.'*

∞∞

TWENTY-EIGHT

Preparing for War

This came as no surprise, however, the shock of its authentication shook all of us. Some years had passed since our victory over the seven warships which tried to initiate an invasion of Hera-soter and the graves of the enemy combatants still remained under the trees at the edge of the village. With the passage of time the possibility of a Crustan invasion seemed less likely, a notion which quickly dispelled, the instant the enemy presence had been detected. With the Sprack rebellion over, further plans, for the defense of our planet, could now be devised. But if the truth be told, there did not appear much more we could do other than fortify our positions, with two more antimatter canons. The village could not supply power for any more than four of these strategic weapons.

Carla rubbed her tummy gently with one hand as she stood beside me. I leaned forward in the chair to inspect the finer telemetry within the hologram. The billions of kilometers ticked off at a terrifying speed, dissipating the distance between the attack force and the planet.

"How long, hon?"

"About forty-two hours," I said.

"We could have packed all the woman and children onto the PE and left."

I looked up at her face. Lines of stress coursed across her forehead. "They have a much greater speed capability and would easily catch up within days. We can't run away from this fight, hon."

She sighed. "I know—just wishful thinking."

"We'll have to wait and see what they do on their arrival. Due to the thickness of the atmosphere they need to get close before firing their nukes. I expect they will soften us up and then demand our surrender."

"What will we do?" she asked.

I didn't answer immediately but turned and put my arms around her waist. Seated in the chair brought my head to the height of her slightly extended motherhood and I kissed the top of her bosom. She understood that I really did not have an answer to the Crustan dilemma. I looked up into her eyes. "We'll give a good account of ourselves but the odds depend on their numbers."

The black cloud on the hologram did not bode well for a small number of enemy craft.

"The forest dwellers have reluctantly moved out of the immediate area and the village folk will hide in the safe places, as they did the last time. Lieutenant Sparkle will control the antimatter canons which will certainly do a lot of damage but we can't protect their positions." I said.

"What about Ozzy?" she asked.

"Ozzy has not been here since before the arrival of the Prime Endeavor and the emergency transmitter is not working either. He would not be able to help us anyway—this is something we must face alone."

She closed her eyes and kissed the top of my head. "We do have a chance, though, don't we?"

"Mike Hunter and his fighters are ready to protect the village, alongside our three androids. All the hand-laser armaments from the PE are at our disposal—we will fight to the last person. I need to have you in a safe place, though," I said.

"I am not leaving your side, hon. Give me a laser and I will do my bit."

I saw the look. There would be no dissuading her and I let it go.

Mickey's velvet voice interrupted our discussion. 'I have a number, Mr. Chairman. It is an overwhelming force—one hundred and ten destroyer class ships, similar to the ones we destroyed on their first attempt and twenty troop carriers.'

I felt weak at the knees. "When will they be in range of our cannons?"

'Thirty-eight hours, Mr. Chairman.'

"Based on our passed experience, what would be the best action to take?"

'I have linked up with the PE's D2000 processor and fed in all the details of our conflicts with the Crustans, Mr. Chairman. In consideration of their overwhelming numbers we should wait to see if they fire on us first. We think they might send an envoy to demand an immediate surrender while keeping their fleet out of range.'

"I doubt whether receiving an envoy will be beneficial to us in any way, but so be it—we'll wait."

*

The three androids, Carla, Mike Hunter and I, all crammed around the console in the command pod, to discuss defense tactics. At the first sign of aggression Happydoo would lead the village people into the cave systems. Due to the distance, with regards to the speed of a hostile missile, we would have time to initiate the evacuation. The Prime Endeavor now resided in a new position, a ravine at the base of a mountain, about twenty-five kilometers away. Our plan involved its use but as a last resort, if the aliens destroyed the antimatter cannons. Rebecca and Philip waited for my order to bring the PE into the fight if I thought it necessary.

The Crustans might destroy the Andromeda as a show of force, a regrettable possibility, but one

I could live with. The androids would remain in the command pod with Carla and I, until the enemy advanced into the quadrangle. Mike Hunter's people, armed with laser-rifles ensconced themselves amongst the village homes plus twenty well trained men and women hidden in foxholes, around the outside perimeter of the pod. This would be our last line of defense. The plan emulated our first experience of the last enemy attack and in addition, the protective field over the quad area had proved its effectiveness, despite the extensive power of the enemy's ordinance.

Mickey kept us updated on the enemy's progress. 'The fleet has slowed down and appears to have entered a wide orbit of the planet, Mr. Chairman. I detect a single vessel on its way, heading straight for us. It looks as though they may first try to intimidate us with threats.'

"They can bring it on. I assume the D2000 is updated with the Crustan's language?"

'Should my communication powers fail the androids will be able to translate for you, boss.'

"Is all connected in the bunker, Lieutenant?"

Sparkle's eyes flashed blue. 'The auxiliary console is ready, Mr. Chairman. If all else fails the enemy might not detect you and Mrs. Conroy.'

"—and you will handle the antimatter canons from here as you did initially?"

'It will be my pleasure, Sir but should the enemy reach the quadrangle as they did last time I will need to leave the pod, to join in the fight with the others. If the canons are still in operation they will be placed under Mickey's command.'

"We must realize the canons will be detected and targeted early on when the enemy ships start dissolving in space—it will only be possible to take several fighters out before they detect where the beams are coming from," said Carla.

"We'll do the best we can. Four canons can cover a formidable area of space. How many of the enemy craft did you say were troop carriers, Mickey?"

'Twenty vessels, which I assume will be carrying combatants, Mr. Chairman. In the previous attack, four of their craft carried sixteen soldiers each. If we do the simple math we could have about three-hundred and sixty to deal with on the ground.'

"Shit—they mean business this time," I said.

We waited. An hour later Mickey updated us again. 'The single enemy craft is entering an orbit within the atmosphere, Mr. Chairman. Their approach will be from the other side of the planet—I suspect they are leery of coming in from an area we might patrol with our weapons.'

"I guess we can expect a communication at any moment," said Carla.

Her intuition cashed in, right on the money. A moment later Mickey activated the holo-receiver and the form of a Crustan stared intently at us. His cruel snout opened in a half-grin and the fiery, red eyes glinted in the light of the craft's internal luminescence.

"This is Crabul Bacture Crish, commander of the scythe destroyer, Burrill. I want to speak to the human, who calls himself, Beckett Conroy."

I rose out of my seat so the holo-camera could pick up my entire body. "This is Beckett Conroy speaking. Please state your business, Commander Crish."

The Crustan's eyes lit up even brighter than before. It appeared the internals of his ship contained a moist atmosphere and I could see rivulets of liquid running down the alien's face and body. The cape around the shoulders appeared impervious to saturation and it hung down the full length of his frame.

"I think you know our business, human, Beckett Conroy. You destroyed several of our ships and we have returned to take retribution."

∞∞

TWENTY-NINE

The Alien's Attack

The alien commander's comment confirmed what we already knew. I tried to sound as casual as possible. "Your presence is not welcome, Commander. We are prepared to resist your attempts to crush our colony."

The alien lowered his snout and glared at us. "Resistance will be futile, human. I have a fleet of over a hundred warships and more than three hundred soldiers, which we will deploy if you do not acquiesce to our demands."

"What demands, Commander."

"You will lay down your weapons and submit to our King. We will take over this planet and you will be our prisoners."

An angry resolve overtook my calm mien. This arrogant son of a bitch would not lay down the law to me.

"We are not easily frightened, Commander Crish. Let me set down my own demands of you and your king. Your fleet must leave this solar system, post haste, or risk being destroyed in the same manner we destroyed your colleagues."

The alien's snout lifted to reveal rows of jagged teeth in a defiant sneer. "You have made a bad choice, human. Prepare to be extinguished from the face of this planet."

The hologram dissolved and we all stared at the empty receiver. No one spoke for a minute or two, until Lieutenant Sparkle gave a chuckle. 'I see the aliens have drawn their line in the sand, Mr. Chairman.'

"Pass the word to the others—we must prepare for an all-out war. Move the people out to the safe places and target the first alien ships that enter within range," I said.

Happydoo left to lead the people out of the village while Mike Hunter and Chief Spanner joined the guards around the perimeter of the quadrangle. Lieutenant Sparkle, Carla and I, moved into the bunker beneath the pod to take up our positions at the auxiliary console.

"Bring up the alien fleet on the holo, Mickey."

The receiver sprung to life and a picture of the enemy formation materialized. Commander Crish's craft grew smaller as it left the atmosphere and sped towards the safety of the fleet. The colony's future existence now hung in the balance.

'The fleet is on the move, Mr. Chairman. I believe the aliens will approach our position after entering the atmosphere on the dark side of the planet. They will destroy the Andromeda as soon as it's spotted but we will at least receive a broadcast regarding the direction of their approach.'

Lieutenant Sparkle settled on a chair in front of the weapons control panel and linked his processor to a port. His unique brain, the D2000, would take charge of the weapon's system to guide the destruction of enemy ships.

I turned to Carla. "All we can do now is wait."

We sat beside the android with our eyes glued to the holo. The aliens disappeared from view to reappear on the opposite side of the planet, picked up by the Andromeda's sensors and beamed via a micro satellite system, to the command pod. The armada turned toward Hera-soter and made its approach. Sparkle waited for the first nuke to be fired from the forward line of enemy ships and when the Andromeda's alarms shrieked he initiated the four forward bow-turrets and fired all the remaining computer-guided missiles. The nukes, guided by the ship's auxiliary control computer, would switch to their own individual sensors, after the Andromeda ceased to exist.

The holo lit up with a flash of light and went dead as the transmission ended. A deep sadness engulfed me. The vessel had been our home for many years prior our arrival on the beautiful planet and it seemed like the death of a living being. Carla gripped my arm and burrowed her face into my neck. The Andromeda had performed its final task—a snapshot of the lead ships entering the atmosphere at a forty-five degree angle, which revealed the direction from where the fleet would approach the colony. This would be enough for Sparkle to align the four antimatter cannons.

We would never know if any of the Andromeda's nukes found their targets. We prepared to face the first salvo of the enemy's ordinance about to be unleashed on their approach. A second later the enemy appeared back on the holographic display and zoomed toward the village at a terrifying speed. The antimatter canons poured out their deathly beams and the lead warships all flying abreast of each other, melted under the annihilation of the antimatter reaction.

The ships behind their spear-head group picked up the position of our cannons and turned their weapons on the fortified turrets situated on top of the two closest mountains. The enemy's initial aim, fraught with the difficulty of speed and surprise missed the turrets and Sparkle managed to knock down eight of the warships within as many seconds, before the aliens gained a lock on the cannon's positions. To exacerbate our plight another wave of warships attacked from a different direction, drawing our cannon fire from the main group, of which several craft managed to avoid destruction. These ships all unleashed their ordinance at the village. Many of the homes around us exploded into fireballs of light and we felt the shockwaves from their direct hits on the protective force-field, which covered the command pod area.

Mike Hunter's people had expected the homes to be the first of our buildings to be demolished and all lay spread out in foxholes around the edge of the quadrangle. I could only hope these advanced provisions would protect our fighters as they would be needed in the final attack by the enemy ground force. Once the Crustans established the extent of our defenses and overcame the cannons they would land close by to finish us off with troops. Sparkle muttered to himself as the holo revealed the destruction of the first antimatter cannon and then the second. The remaining cannons continued to target the warships as they flew between the mountains with greater evasive ability but within minutes our antimatter defense system lay in ruins.

Lieutenant Sparkle sat back from the panel. *I'm afraid that is as far as our antimatter defense can go. The enemy will soon realize we have no other major weapons and decide to land their troops. I must get out of the pod and join Mr. Hunter's group.'*

"Mickey will keep me abreast of matters until the enemy destroys our transmitters. You and Chief Spanner need to keep a constant video transmission to the pod so I can see how things are faring on ground level. How many warships did we destroy?"

'Only twelve, Mr. Chairman. I suspect the carriers will have already landed at Abrams Lake.'

To confirm his suspicion he switched to the cameras which fielded a view of the lake. Large carriers descended on the stretch of open ground which once housed the Prime Endeavor. Two of the behemoths, already settled, spewed out combatants. The troops formed up in lines and waited for their leader's instructions to invade the village.

"Happydoo will have settled all our people in the safe places by now and should be on his way back to join us. You three androids are our last bid at an offense—make the best of it."

'It has been a pleasure to serve, Mr. Chairman. We will do our best.'

He climbed the bunker's ladder and disappeared through the trapdoor into the command pod above. Carla and I settled at the console to view the coming battle for as long as transmission lasted.

"Give me a 360 please, Mickey."

'Aye, aye boss.'

The holo changed to an overhead view of the pod and its surroundings. I could see up to the lake and the base areas of both mountains. Carla took hold of a laser-rifle and held it against her bosom. I placed my hand on her tummy and felt the baby kick.

"I guess we'll all go down fighting," I said.

"Let's see how our guards have handled the warship attack."

Mickey zoomed the holo down to the positions in the quadrangle, where Mike Hunter's fighters had dug in and we could see their positions with clarity. All seemed to have survived the initial onslaught of the enemy. The group on the perimeter of the pod, untouched by the shock-waves precipitated by the enemy's bombs, waited with lasers at the ready. I perceived the enemy did not want to mete out wholesale destruction of the colony. From my previous knowledge of the Crustan's, they enjoyed taken prisoners for the purpose of sport. This may have been their greatest mistake. I did not think they knew of the android deterrent and we would make good use of this capability, by drawing the enemy into close quarter combat, where the droid's lasers could do immeasurable damage.

I could no longer hear the swoosh of enemy fighters overhead and I assumed the fleet must have been sent back into orbit to wait. The warships would be a final backup to the ground troop assault, should it fail. The enemy combatants advanced on our position and fanned out to surround the village perimeter. No communication came from Happydoo and I wondered at his status. The holo showed the enemy advance, through the roads of the village, their steady deliberate progress a mark of a disciplined, tactical force. I knew Mike Hunter, his guards and Chief Spanner waited, in anticipation of Lieutenant Sparkle's order, to open fire. By the enemy's position I could see the anticipated action from our group appeared to be imminent.

The enemy advance reached the open area between the homes and the quadrangle. As the first line of Crustans broke the cover of the buildings and moved toward the command pod Lieutenant Sparkle gave his order to fire. The guards stood up in their foxholes and poured laser beams into the oncoming group of combatants. The lieutenant commanded a 360 degree view through the camera feed from Mickey's system—the same feed I received on my holo-receiver in the bunker. The enemy's advance, orchestrated in a semicircle towards the command pod as the final target, suffered the laser blast for but a moment. As Crustans fell to the ground in puffs of smoke, more came up from behind, to fire their weapons at our guards, who instinctively ducked back into the holes for protection. At that moment I heard a single enemy warship as at it dived on the pod, seconds before the holo image went blank. I experienced a moment's lapse in my thoughts and my eyes closed for a brief second.

Carla and I glanced at each other. We both felt the effect of some force which swept through the bunker.

"What was that," she asked.

∞∞

THIRTY

The End is Near

I hesitated as all the alarms on the console went off simultaneously.

"I believe we've lost the video feed," I said.

The illumination inside the bunker dimmed as the emergency backup power kicked in.

"It looks as though we've lost all our power, except the auxiliary water feed to the reactor," she said. I looked at the console readouts and confirmed her suspicions.

"At least it won't overheat but as far as visual contact with the outside world, we're done."

No sound leaked through into the bunker and for the first time I considered our end to be near.

The holo-receiver sprang to life with a hazy image. We had a sudden view of the outside surroundings.

'Master Beckett? Are you and Mrs. Carla still there?'

I breathed a moment's sigh of relief—Happydoo.

"Where are you," I asked.

'I am standing on a hillock at the farm, Master Beckett—where I have a view of the proceedings. I did not arrive in time to join the fight.'

"What has happened? We heard a warship fly overhead and then our holo went blank."

'The warship unleashed some sort of field over the quadrangle, Master Beckett. Our guards all appear to have succumbed to it. Whatever its nature, the beam must wield a power to stun the human mind. Lieutenant Sparkle and Chief Spanner also seemed to have been neutralized. The command pod, above you, is still intact. I believe the graphene floor of the pod must have saved you from the effects.'

"Now I know what that strange sensation was. It almost caused me to black out but then it passed."

'The enemy force has surrounded the pod, Master Beckett. I suggest you and Mrs. Carla sit tight. I will try to sneak up and see if there is anything I can do.'

"Be careful, my friend."

'I will keep my feed to the pod's holo-receiver going, Master Beckett. You will be able to see what happens.'

Carla and I waited for what seemed an eternity. We watched as my valet crept closer to the battle area. His video feed kept us informed of the status and it became clear we faced an imminent defeat. I did not know if Mike Hunter and his people were still alive. Some of our guards lay sprawled half in and half out of their foxholes while others lay crumpled, their faces out of sight. I shuddered to think of what sort of weapon the enemy had deployed to take out everyone so efficiently and quickly. Happydoo now lay on the ground at the edge of the homes. He could not advance any further without being spotted. The warship flew overhead, back and forth, its commander looking for any sign of retaliation from the command pod.

"What are we going to do, hon?"

Carla's calmness in the face of the odds helped me to keep my composure. "I'll fight off anyone who tries to come through that trapdoor," I said. "I love you, babe—"

Happydoo kept up a commentary of the enemy's status. In the hologram we saw the Crustans stop in a circle around the pod. Our guards in the perimeter had all fared the same as those in the quadrangle, all incapacitated and inert within their foxholes. The Commander of the force disappeared through the pod's front entrance and I pulled Carla to the wall behind the console. We both held the laser-rifles at the ready and waited.

The Crustan commander stomped around on the pod floor like an ancient mammoth. He either possessed an infra-red heat seeker or he figured it out because the trapdoor lifted and I caught a view of the infamous snout and fiery red eyes. I'm not sure if those eyes mesmerized me, or I froze—I couldn't activate the laser trigger. Carla came to my rescue and squeezed off a shot which went wide of the mark. I could see the arrogance of the enemy who didn't even flinch at the beam, which singed the edge of the trapdoor. The Crustan stared at us and in that instant I saw a green flash light up the inside of the pod. The brightness of it blinded me for a moment as I activated my laser-rifle and fired off a beam. When my eyes opened again the Crustan had disappeared.

I glanced at the holo which still danced on the receiver, as seen through the android's camera eyes. To my consternation, the entire area remained aglow with a greenish colored hue. We heard explosions emanate from the quadrangle and the guttural sounds of the alien's in distress.

"Happydoo—are you still there?" I asked.

For several moments the android did not answer but when he did his voice elevated an octave.

'You are not going to believe this, Master Beckett.'

My hopes soared. "Try me."

'You can leave the bunker now, Master Beckett, and see for yourself.'

I grabbed Carla's arm and pulled her toward the ladder. She clambered up with me in close pursuit and we stopped at the door of the pod. The entire area remained lit up under a ghostly greenish glow and dead Crustan combatants lay everywhere in the quadrangle. A huge gray shape hovered over the top of the command pod and as I looked beyond it into the darkness of the sky, I saw green beams and yellow flashes of light, all over the heavens. Confusion reigned in my mind and I stared at the scene without comprehension.

Carla stood beside me also, captivated by the strange sight. "I've never seen craft like that, hon. I wonder who they are."

Explosions erupted far out into space as a tremendous battle took place before our eyes. Happydoo plodded toward us, his blue orbs oscillating in excitement. I heard a familiar sound across the top of the trees, from the direction of Abrams Lake and a small craft zoomed overhead, to land on the far side of the quadrangle. I recognized the compact contraption. Even before the hatch opened I knew who our rescuer was—Ozzy stepped down onto the red grass. In my life, many transcending moments came to mind, but this one eclipsed them all. We ran out to greet our alien friend.

"Dear boy, dear boy, dear boy. How wonderful to see you two again—how are you keeping, Carla, my dear."

Ozzy's condom shaped body vibrated with pleasure as he glided up to us and stretched out his sets of stubby limbs. I could no longer contain myself and tears of relief flowed down my cheeks.

"You certainly cut things fine, Ozzy," I said.

"You know I would never let you and Carla down, dear boy."

"How did you know about our plight?" Carla asked.

Our intelligence informed the Lumbrian controlling body that an armada of Crustan ships had slipped into the universe from the Crustan dimension. With much pressure from me our overlords consented to stop the enemy from taking over and I guess we got here in the nick of time—and what is this I see, Carla, my dear?"

He indicated her slightly extended abdomen. "Is there a baby to be born soon?"

She laughed. "Thanks to you, Ozzy, this baby will be born. If you had been an hour later we would have all been dead."

The alien farted and belched air. "I am delighted, for you and Beckett, my dear."

I looked skyward again. "I see your fleet is taking it to the enemy."

"Have no fear, dear boy. The enemy is no match for this force. It's the best we have in the Lumbrian dimension. I doubt if they will ever attempt this type of thing again."

Carla looked with concern at the foxholes where many of our guards could be seen, still inert. "We must attend to our wounded."

"The Lumbrian physicians will take care of it," said Ozzy. He spoke into a tiny transmitter tied to one of his wrists and the large grey craft overhead slowly settled down beside the Orbitron. The hatch opened and several Ozzy-like aliens sailed down to the ground and headed our way. Ozzy floated over to one of them and pointed to the foxholes around the quad perimeter. He called another and indicated those close to the pod. Each alien carried a shiny case which I assumed contained all the substances required for healing our injured.

The Lumbrian rejoined us. "Let's find a place to settle your nerves while the physicians do their work."

∞∞

THIRTY-ONE

A Miraculous Event

The physicians made short work of the re-suscitation process. Ozzy gave us the good news. "It seems the Crustan commander wanted to keep you all alive for their sporting activities. They would have transported you to their dimension to parade their victory before the king and then made sport by pitting you against some of their weird animal life."

I explained we were not prepared to be taken alive. Ozzy mumbled sympathetically but I could see he thought the Crustans would have devised a plan not to kill us.

"I believe they were going to extend their operations in your universe to enslave all the thousands of civilizations within ten thousand lightyears of Hera-soter. The Lumbrian Controlling Body considers your universe to be unique and should not be interfered with from other dimensions. It took some persuasion on my behalf, to convince them the Crustans were intent on taking it over for themselves," said Ozzy.

"Well, I'm so glad you did. We would not have survived this onslaught. We'll have to strengthen our defenses immeasurably in case they try again," I said.

Ozzy farted more air. "They will know we are watching. The war between our two dimensions is coming to a close. There might even be a truce and I will definitely push for them to stay out of our seed dimensions."

Mike Hunter and his brave guards all recovered from the knock-out blow delivered by the Crustans. The processors of Lieutenant Sparkle and Chief Spanner required descrambling but at the conclusion of the procedure, both carried on their daily routines with added vigor. The colony returned to normal and several months later two occasions featured to bring joy to everyone's hearts —the birth of our son, Raymond, and an alert from Mickey on the arrival of the third mission from Earth.

One day, lieutenant Sparkle and I walked out to the farm together on an excursion to check the security of our crops. "Okay, Sparkle—things seemed to have settled down now in the colony and we have some time on our hands. Tell me how you escaped that blast when you were checking out the derelict Crustan ship?"

This question referred to the time, on our journey, when the Crustans first attacked us. They vacated their damaged warship and mined it for the purpose of killing any inquisitive humans. Sparkle had been the volunteer who offered to check the vessel out. His boarding of the vessel activated the planted bomb and the warship disintegrated. Somehow the lieutenant, whom we thought to have been destroyed in the blast, survived and made it back to the Andromeda at the time when the second Crustan vessel dispatched a party to board us. The question of his survival still plagued me and I could see no reason for the android to avoid the question this time.

Sparkle screwed up his synthetic skin into a cheeky grin and glanced at me. *'This question really bothers you, Mr. Chairman?'*

"Yes—I understand unanswered questions might be lost on you droids but I'm human—I need to know."

'Alright, Sir, I'll tell you, since you insist. When you saw the video breakdown you thought the explosion had taken place, but it hadn't. I tripped and bashed the front of my face against the floor, moments before I reached the door, disrupting the camera's vision. For several seconds my vision became marred and I stumbled out of the warship's hatch into the EEP. The canopy closed automatically and that's when the bomb went off. The blast flung the EEP away from the vessel and my processor suffered a technical problem which took several years to repair itself.'

I finished the story for him. "—and when your processor came back online you made it back to the Andromeda to see the enemy boarding us?"

'That's correct, Sir.'

"Why couldn't you have told me this when I first asked you?"

'Call it techno-pride, Mr. Chairman.'

I shook my head and laughed. "Well now I've heard everything. Isn't pride an emotion, Lieutenant?"

'You may link the two, Sir.'

"The next thing you'll probably want is to have a good cry about it," I said.

Sparkle chuckled. *'It will have to be a dry one, Mr. Chairman.'*

*

Carla sat on the bed breastfeeding young Raymond. I couldn't believe how seldom the boy cried and he always seemed to be content. The return to normality allowed us more time at home, to spend with our newborn and to build family values. Happydoo spent much of his time helping Carla with household chores and babysitting when we needed a little time for ourselves.

I asked the android what he thought about being an uncle. His answer came as no surprise to us.

'I would be happy to be Raymond's uncle, Master Beckett but is an uncle not supposed to be a human, blood relative of a child?'

"Not really—providing we don't get too technical," I said.

'But don't you think he should know I'm just a machine, Master Beckett?'

I thought about it for a moment. "You could always tell him you're his techno-uncle."

The android forced a broad grin and gave a chuckle, followed by the pirouette and foot-stomp routine. I hoped Raymond would come to appreciate the Happydoo as much as his ancestors did.

My dad and Freda visited on a regular basis and we often resorted to Earth-talk. We would discuss the differences of our new lifestyle, in comparison to our home planet and how we should guide the development of our society. Conroy senior talked about building a lab to continue his penchant for genetics and the study of Eugenics, a subject which had the twentieth century in an uproar. He believed, to a degree, we could eliminate much of the human deficiencies by selective breeding, but on this we disagreed.

"I can't not see our colony accepting such a socially degrading system to improve the genepool. I believe a better course of action would be to continue to resolve the problems currently entrenched in the human genome. To do this more efficiently there is the need to develop a nano DNA repair system, a process I would love to work on, personally."

My dad smiled. "This would be a fulltime venture and your chairmanship of the committee would need to be handed over to someone else."

I realized his motive for bringing up the Eugenics thing. He wasn't really for such a course of action—he wanted to test my resolve to get back into genetic engineering.

"I'm sure my replacement on the committee could be arranged and my guess is, you would love to be involved—right?"

"Right. I believe there is still so much more we can achieve together," he said.

∞∞

EPILOGUE

Dr. Beckett Conroy.
Executive Chairman,
Hera-soter Establishment Committee.
　　02-30-07. FE :　　Project　Establishment Log.

The Star Voyager, under the command of President Commander, Brian Gibson, arrived today at 11:34 am. With a total compliment of Three-thousand, four-hundred and twelve, our colony now increases to Sixty-six hundred and fifty-seven humans, plus seven androids. Included in this number are twenty-seven children. Today is my last day as chairman of the Establishment Committee and I will be retiring to continue the quest for longevity.

The End

∞∞∞

MORE BOOKS BY COLIN SETTEFIELD

The Helium-3 Conspiracy

Love Sweat tears

Subduction Zone

*The A-Mortal Gene (Survival of a Species Trilogy)

*The habitat Relocation Project (Survival of a Species Trilogy)

Survival Of A Species Trilogy (3 books in One)

The Memory Hunter.   Special Agent O'Malley

Merlin's War SpeciaL Agent O'Malley

The Omega File Special Agent O'Malley

Operation Terra Firma Special Agent O'Malley